GREEN MAMBA: THE COMPLETE
CASES OF DAFFY DILL, VOLUME 2

BOOKS IN THE ARGOSY LIBRARY:

GREEN MAMBA
THE COMPLETE CASES OF DAFFY DILL, VOLUME 2

RICHARD B. SALE

ILLUSTRATED BY
JOSEPH A. FARREN

COVER BY
WALTER DE MARIS

POPULAR PUBLICATIONS · 2024

TABLE OF CONTENTS

THE BUMPER-OFFER

*Only Three Lines of Newsprint—but
They Advertised One Crime, Caused a
Second, and Put Daffy Dill on the Spot*

1

KILLING NEWS

THE SCENE WAS a night club in the daytime. Now the only time a guy goes to a night club in the daytime is because he feels thirsty and because he is generally fed up with civilization. There are no dancing dames in the daytime. There is no swanky food either. There is only a long polished bar with lots of bottles and glasses, a short Irish bartender named Shorty McGinnis with a bald dome that gleams like the midnight sun, and a hand—McGinnis' very own—which has never lost its touch.

He slid my Old-fashioned across to me, grinning as he said: "Drinks may come and go, Daffy, but I'll bet this charge is the tastiest you ever guzzled, either here in the Hideaway Club or any place else on the main stem."

"Well," I said, "I dunno, Shorty." I was remembering the time someone handed me a spiked Daiquiri in the old Three Penny Club, a speak which Vinnie Dunner used to operate in the pre-repeal days. I lifted the Old-fashioned. "Anyway, Shorty, here's hair on your head. Long may it wave!"

I had just gotten the first mouthful down my throat when a hand fell on my crooked arm. I glanced around. It was Bill Latham, my old pal, who owns and runs the Hideaway and is a pretty swell guy, unless you owe him money. Then he's a china egg.

"Listen, Daffy," he said.

"Listen yourself, toots," I said, cutting him off. "Didn't anyone ever tell you the futility of it?"

Latham frowned. He looked pretty serious. "The futility of what?"

"Of stopping Daffy Dill when he was drinking an Old-fashioned?" I shook my head. "Yea, verily, Bill, it's more futile than trying to stop a tiger's charge."

"No time for jokes, Daffy," he said, without smiling. "Come on into my office." He turned and started for his private door.

"Hey!" I said. "Wait'll I finish this thing!"

"Finish it in here," Latham said tersely. "Someone wants you on the phone. If he wants you about what I think he does it's pretty serious. Make it fast!"

I sighed. "Shorty—that's life. Business always coming before pleasure. Save this for me. I'll be back, and that's a threat."

I turned and left the bar, and I went into Bill Latham's private office, which same is no mean job of modernistic furnishing. I grabbed a chair next to his desk as he tossed the handset to me. I covered the mouthpiece and said:

"Who is it, Bill, the Old Man?"

He shook his head, frowning. "It's LaVerne."

"LaVerne?"

"For God's sake!" Latham exclaimed. "It's Jimmy LaVerne of the Town Club, that gambling spot on Forty-fifth. Don't tell me you've never been there!"

"Sure," I said. "But why should LaVerne phone me?"

I fired at
Torkey twice

"Answer him," snapped Latham, "and see."

"And why," I asked, ignoring the crack, "should *you* have the jitters?"

"You'd have the jitters, too," Latham replied sharply. "It's just like suicide, the damn fool. Talk to LaVerne!"

I uncovered the mouthpiece, wondering what in hell it was all about. I said, "Hello, Jimmy. This is Daffy Dill, alive and well. So what's the gag, and where's the body?"

"No gag," LaVerne said in a steely voice. "Now listen, Daffy, and no smart cracks on the side. You know Harry Lyons, don't you?"

"I avoid him," I said.

"But you know him, don't you? You must. He works on

that same rag as you do, the *Chronicle*. He has that wise-cracking colyum, *Read Between the Lyons*."

"So what?" I asked. I knew Harry Lyons, all right. We got along like a mongoose and a cobra. He was the so-and-so who fixed libel on a feature I wrote on Adolph, the chef of the Grenada Hotel, which same got me canned. I had to solve a kidnaping to get my job back, consequently I sent him no orchids. He had finally persuaded the Old Man to give him a daily colyum of garbage on which movie star was living with which, and which big-shot was paramouring whom, and a lot of other stuff that makes a bad odor.

LaVerne said, "Can you get hold of him, Daffy?"

"Maybe so," I replied. "What for?"

"Never mind what for. Just get hold of him. Tell him to take a powder for Cuba, Mexico or Europe. Tell him to get out of the country. Otherwise his chances are nil. He can come back when it's all over."

"Say—what is this?"

"And remember, this is all off-record. Forget I called you."

"But—"

I started. Then I stopped. I heard a click as LaVerne hung up and there I was holding a dead wire. I stared at the handset for a second, sort of stunned.

Latham nervously lighted a cigarette and glanced at me. "What'd he say?"

"Well, I can't make heads or tails of it," I said. "He wants me to get hold of Harry Lyons and tell Lyons to blow town. To blow the country, in fact. I don't make it out at all."

LATHAM SHOOK HIS head. He looked solemn. "I thought

this might happen. Lyons is a fool. He must've been pie-eyed to take such a chance. And Jimmy LaVerne is the man who ought to know."

I sat back in the chair, took off my hat, and pulled at my hair. "Listen, friend," I said, wild-eyed, "will you let me in on all this hocus-pocus. What's the matter with Lyons anyway?"

"For a newspaper man," Latham replied sarcastically, "you read less than any other human being." He dug into a pile of papers on top of his desk, located one, and handed it to me. It was a home edition of the *Chronicle*, my own sheet.

I said, "You mean you want me to read this? Puleeze, Bill, I have to write for it to make a living, but I don't have to read it."

"Nix," Latham snapped. "Take a peek at Harry Lyons' colyum for today and let yourself in on the mystery."

"Oh," I said. I took the paper from him and thumbed through the second section until I came to the feature page. This page carries one or two cartoons, a book-chat colyum, a political colyum, and Harry Lyons' gem of chitter-chatter on what's happening under-handedly for the day. "Do I have to wade through all of it," I asked, "or can you give me a hint?"

"Somewhere in the second paragraph," said Latham. "It's headed 'Goings On Around The Town.'"

"A very original subtitle," I remarked, "which Lyons no doubt lifted from Odd McIntyre or Walter Winchell. Now, lemme see...."

I found the second paragraph and read through it. About the middle of it I came across the sore spot. It nearly knocked me for a loop. I've written news for a long, long time, but it jarred me to see news like that actually in print.

Lyons' colyum went like this:

This afternoon, in the heat of the day, Vinnie (Killer) Dunner, the biggest beer baron of the BR days (Before Repeal), will be neatly kicked in by a well-known hood from out Detroit way. Orchids to the bumper-offer for cleaning our fair city of a rat.

I whistled. "Holy, holy, holy!" I said. "He must be nuts! If somebody really bumps Vinnie Dunner, Lyons is on a spot himself!"

"Yeah," said Latham. "And now you know why I've got the jitters. Lyons is a pretty good kid, outside of being a smart-aleck like you. He's trying to scoop the world on this and he's broken through pretty thin ice. It ain't pleasant to sit here waiting for the word."

"The word?" I said. "You mean—Lyons' obit?"

Latham nodded.

"Hell," I said. "There's still time, isn't there? How about this, Bill? Know anything about Dunner? Is he really on the spot?"

"He won't eat tonight, Daffy," Latham said. "I know. Got it first-class over the grapevine. He's through. And I'm pretty sure that if the bumper-offer sees Lyons' chatter—well, look at it yourself. If you were the hood, you'd be wondering pretty hard how much Lyons knew. And instead of waiting to find out, you'd bullet Lyons to close his mouth."

I grabbed the phone without a word and quickly called

the *Chronicle* office. Dinah Mason, the beauteous and platinum-haired Garbo of my life, answered.

"Listen, angel-eyes," I said tersely, "is Harry Lyons in the office?"

"No," she said. "What's the matter, toots? You sound diabetic."

"Do you know where he's gone?"

"No," she said. "And why don't you two kiss and make up instead of scrapping all the time? I suppose he's done something now that makes you want to lay eggs on his skull with a hammer."

"Listen, Dinah," I said earnestly. "This is no kid, get me? Lyons is on the spot. Understand? He'll be knocked off if I don't—"

"Hold it, Daffy!" she exclaimed suddenly. "It's a call from Sampson on the open wire to the chief." I could hear her plug a jack and I waited for a few seconds. Then she was right back at me. "Hi-de-ho, scribe!" she cried. "And where is your nose for news? Vinnie Dunner was just machine-gunned on West Forty-second Street near the Eltinge Theater! Sampson got the flash from h.q. He says Hanley is covering for the homicide squad."

"Dinah—for God's sake—listen!" I bellowed. "Harry Lyons is on the spot! Can't you understand me? He prophesied that Dunner would be killed today. And now you just told me Dunner's gone—"

Latham leaped to his feet. "Vinnie bumped?" he snapped.

I nodded, getting purple. "Listen, Dinah! I've got to find Lyons. He doesn't know what it's all about. He's got to lam or he's next! See if any of the boys—"

"Sit tight," she said coolly. "I get you." She was gone for

about a minute. All the time Latham kept puffing furiously at his cigarette and I sweated away four pounds. Finally she came back and she didn't waste words either. Her voice was as taut as a fiddle-string.

"MacGuire has a lead, Daffy. He says Lyons was a little tight when he left. That was around one o'clock. Lyons said he was going uptown for lunch. He hangs out at the King's Highway restaurant. I hope you find him."

I hung up without reply. Latham crushed his cigarette in a tray and clipped, "Know where he is?"

"Prowling," I said. "I'm going to make a try. Thanks, Bill. I'll let you know." I jammed on my hat and skidded out of the private office. Short McGinnis stared at me as I ran for the door.

"Daffy!" he yelled. "How about this Old-fashioned?"

"Burn it," I said. "I'm in a hurry!"

2

THE THIRTY BLACK FLIES

THE GAL BEHIND the counter of the King's Highway restaurant was a looker. "Sure," she said, "I know Harry Lyons. What's it to yuh?"

"Nix on the baby-stare, sister," I said. "I want info from you and only info, get me? He isn't here now, is he?"

"Say," she said, "yuh're pretty fresh, mister."

"I'll say I am," I growled at her. "Fresh enough to lay a duster over one of those bedroom orbs of yours. I'm asking you—where's Lyons now?"

"He left," she said. "He was eatin' when a flash came over the radio. Yuh know—about Vinnie Dunner's kick-in. When he heard that, Harry just got up. 'Baby,' he says to me, 'I've scooped 'em all this time!' Then he pays the check and lams."

That was enough for me. I skipped out of the restaurant and went racing down Broadway. If you ever want to perform a miracle, try running down the main stem. If the crowd doesn't stop you, every flatfoot along the route thinks you're a dip making a break.

I had pretty good luck. I made Forty-second Street in record time and turned right, going west on it. Down near the Eltinge Theater on the opposite side of the street a couple of mounted cops were having a sweet time keeping the milling mob back from in front of a small drug store which plainly was the scene of the bump-off. I crossed over and started to swim through them.

When I got near the door three Frankenstein monsters in blue uniforms with voices like bears and nightsticks like telegraph poles started to swing and yell at me in the same breath. I saw right off that my press pass wasn't going to carry any weight with these boys. For a second I was stumped.

Then I remembered the badge I carry on the back of one of my lapels. It's a swell imitation of a detective's shield, and more than once I had used it to get into or out of a tight spot. One of the cops grabbed me, brandishing the club under my nose.

"Mugg!" he roared. "Get the hell outa here!"

I said, "Cut that out," very curtly, and I flashed the badge so quick he couldn't make it out. Then I added, "Is Lieutenant Hanley inside?"

"Yeah," the cop replied. "Yeah, he is. Go on in."

"Okay," I said, and stepped past him.

There were more people inside that peewee drug store than there were outside on the sidewalk. Dicks, patrolmen, Doc Kyne, the chief M.E., who gets sore when I call him the Vulture of Centre Street, two Public Welfare boys all ready to take the corpse for a ride to the morgue. Honestly, the only one missing was gruff Inspector Halloran, commanding the homicide bureau. For a down-and-out beer baron I had to admit that Vinnie Dunner still had the glamor to draw out plenty of the force.

I made out Bill Hanley's homely pan in a few seconds,

head and shoulders over the rest of the crowd. It was serious and lined. I had to smile. Hanley always got upset over the simplest crimes at all. Give him one that was really a honey and he always laughed his way through it, kidding it more or less, until

Daffy Dill

four or five slugs had perforated his hat. Then—bullets are like that—he would begin to take it seriously.

I yelled, "Poppa!"

He turned and saw me. "Com'ere, Daffy," he said.

I pushed my way through the dicks. Now, this drug store was a real dinky. To the left there was a long counter, glassed of course, and filled with medicines and bottles. There remained only about four feet of space in front of the counter for customers to occupy when they made a purchase. And some of this was taken up by a single public telephone booth. That's where Hanley was standing—in front of the booth. When I got to him he nudged me before he spoke and pointed.

I looked down.

Vinnie Dunner lay there, face up, both of his arms raised over his head, his hands tightly clenched.

I whistled. You know, a man never looks quite as dead as when he's been machine-gunned. Did you ever see the

frosting of a white cake with a swarm of black flies all over
it? That's how a man looks when machine gun slugs have
perforated his hide. They had stripped Vinnie's coat off.
His white shirt—in front—was covered with little black
holes, each one looking like a fly and each one covered with
a little blood. There must have been thirty of the things.
They ranged all the way from his belly to his heart, and
there were a couple in his head. He must have taken a full
pound of lead.

"YOU KNOW WHAT happened?" Hanley asked. "This guy—
the killer I mean—walked in here with a violin case. No
one else was in the store except Vinnie, and he was in
the booth making a call. The killer points up to a shelf
behind the storekeeper—he told us this—and asks for
something there. When the poor derp turned around the
killer slugged him. And when the derp came to, Vinnie
was lying right there, perforated." He sighed and shook
his head. "A neat job, too."

"Where's the storekeeper?" I said.

"In the back room," said Hanley. "He's still got the
jitters."

"Can he recognize the bumper-offer?" I asked.

Hanley made a face. "You know how it is—a hundred
guys a day come in to buy. He never even gave the bird
a second look. Doesn't even know what clothes the bird
wore. You covering for the paper, Daffy?"

I jerked guiltily. "By God, no!" I said. "I came here looking for Lyons. Have you seen him?"

"Harry Lyons?" Hanley looked around. "He was here
awhile ago, yelling something about a scoop. One of the
boys started to toss him out, but I let him stay. Maybe he's

in the back room with the
storekeeper. What's the
matter, Daffy?"

"Plentee," I said.
"Thanks, Poppa. I'll see
you later, maybe."

I turned and went into
the back room. It was a
dingy, dirty little cubby-
hole with a couple of
tables and shelves of big
medicine bottles around
the walls, each of them

Bill Hanley

tabbed. The storekeeper was sitting at one of the tables,
white and frightened. He had a bandage around his head.
There were two dicks with him. One of them was Guilfoyle, an operative whom I'd met on cases with Hanley a
couple of times before. He grinned at me.

"Listen, pal," I said, "have you seen Lyons? Harry
Lyons?"

"That big-mouthed colyumist?" Guilfoyle said. "Sure
I seen him. He was in here just a few seconds ago, trying
to bump this poor lug for some info on the killing." He
motioned to the storekeeper. "He left by the back door
there. You can catch him if you run. He's only been gone
a second or two."

Waving my thanks, I went out the back door. It opened
into a shadowy alley—shadowy, that is, in the daytime.
The sun didn't get in much work because of the narrow-
ness of the walk, and it was pretty damp. Left, the alley
was blind, ending in a stone wall. Right, I saw that it

opened on Broadway, just a crevice between two buildings. And framed in that crevice, walking jauntily towards
the sunlight, was Harry Lyons, the man with the skin you
love to clutch.

"Lyons!" I yelled. He stopped short and turned around.
He was a little high. He had a silly grin on his map, and
he looked slender as a pole. His hat was tipped far back on
his head, the way he'd seen reporters in movies wear them.

I ran to him.

"Well, well," he sneered, "if it isn't Dill, the bane of the
Fourth Estate, the *Chronicle's* self-made hero, and the
biggest heel in the racket!"

"Never mind the sweet amenities of life, chump," I said,
grabbing his arm and pulling him back farther into the
alley. "I want a word with you."

He sniffed. "I dunno," he said. "I have to be careful whom
I speak with, you see. I might get a bad name if anyone sees
you with me."

"Yeah," I grated, "and you might get a nice wooden
kimono if you don't shut your trap and listen to what I've
got to say! You're a fool, Harry. You know by now what
news is fit to print and what news isn't. Any newspaperman does. Your cheery little prophecy in that colyum was
the biggest bone-head job you've ever done!"

Lyons laughed in my face. "Boy," he said, "are you burned
up! I guess you don't feel so good when I scoop you, eh?"

"Scoop *me?*" I said. "Listen, you boob, and get this
straight. I don't give two damns about what you print.
Most of the time it's a lot of lying anyhow. But today's gem
I wouldn't have printed for a hundred grand. Do you know
what you've done?"

"Sure," he said, leering. "I printed news that happened after my paper was on the streets. So what?"

"That item," I said, "has put you on the spot."

He stopped laughing and looked at me sharply. "On—the—spot," he said. "You're crazy. What are you trying to do, crab my glory?"

"On the spot," I said. "And that's level. Listen, Harry, you know I hate I your guts. Why should I be standing here telling you this? I was at the Hide-away this noon when Jimmy LaVerne—"

"LaVerne?" Lyons said, his eyes narrowing. He turned a trifle pale. "What about him?"

"LaVerne called me," I said, "and told me to lay hold of you and give you a tip to skip the country until this whole thing blows over."

"But why?" Lyons asked, sort of scared now.

"Don't be a sap," I said. "Your item of chatter indicated that you knew in advance that Vinnie Dunner was going to be rubbed out. The bumper-offer will want to clear up several loose ends. He'll start to figure that maybe you had an 'in' that he was doing the job. He won't wait for you to testify at h.q. He'll cart his violin case around and give you the slug to close your mouth.

"Another thing—as soon as the cops read that colyum, you're going up on the carpet to disclose the source of your news. That isn't going to help the bumper-offer's opinion of you much, either. So that's it. Bill Latham said it. LaVerne said it. Now I say it. Grab the first shuttle West, or hop a freighter and go see Peru. New York is awful unhealthy."

Lyons' mouth was working, his lips drawn and bloodless.

"But, my God, Daffy," he cried. "I don't know who rubbed out Vinnie Dunner!"

"You don't?" I stared at him. "Then how'd you—"

"I WAS AT the Town Club last night," Lyons said, looking furtively up and down the alley. "Jimmy LaVerne's place. I wanted to see Jimmy, but the girl at the hat check said he was in conference and would be for quite awhile. She was sort of funny about it, and I figured LaVerne might have a dame in his office with him. It was good for a colyum item. I sneaked around the side door of his office—you know—over by those palm trees on the dance floor?"

"Keep talking."

"I hit my ear at the keyhole and parked. There was a man in there with LaVerne. I heard LaVerne say:

" 'Just got in from Detroit, eh?' And then this guy with him said:

" 'Yep, Jimmy. I got a little job to do in town. Vinnie Dunner." Then LaVerne said:

" 'Serious?' And the guy from Detroit said:

" 'He played the wheel at my place. In the hole a hundred grand. He welched. Took a powder for New York. I guess he thought I'd forget it. I came right after him, Jimmy. He's through, anyway. It might as well be me who does it.'

"There was a silence for a few seconds. Then LaVerne said:

" 'Can't blame you.' And I didn't hear any more until the guy from Detroit remarked he thought this afternoon would be best. Then I came away."

"Have you got any dough?" I asked.

"Yeah," Lyons said, his voice strained. "But—how do I get it, Daffy? I don't want to go walking around this burg now! If the bumper-offer finds me— Good God, Daffy, we've got to do something. I don't know anything about that murder! I'm clean and I've got to—"

"Pipe down," I said, shaking him. His voice had gotten shrill and he was louder than he realized. I thought for a second. "You've got a checkbook on you?"

"Yeah."

"How much will you need for the run-out?"

"I'd better take—two grand—I guess," Lyons replied shakily.

"Okay," I said. "Write it out to Jimmy LaVerne. You got a pen? Good! Write it out to LaVerne. Then give it to me. After that, you take a cab and go to my place. You know where it is?"

"Yeah, but—"

"No buts. You stick at my place. I'll run over to LaVerne's and cash this check. I'll see what I can do about meeting the Detroit torpedo and talking him out of rubbing you. If it's no go there, I'll get you your tickets on some ship sailing tonight and then I'll go to your apartment, pack your clothes, and send 'em to the ship. Then I'll come to my place, give you the rest of the dough and you can tear for Asia. How's it sound?"

"It'll have to do," Lyons croaked. "Wait a second." He yanked out his checkbook and fountain pen. Then he made me turn around. Using my back as a desk, he hurriedly scribbled a check payable to Jimmy LaVerne for two grand. I took it.

"All right," I said. "Now lam for my spot. I'll see you in around two hours. Maybe less." I gripped his arm. "And keep up your nerve."

We walked out of the alley onto Broadway. Lyons was a trifle white around the gills and his hands were trembling. He went right to the first cab in line by the curb and climbed in. The engine rattled and he was gone uptown.

I took a cab myself. "Town Club," I told the driver. "On Forty-fifth."

"Sure," he said. "I know." He shifted and we went off.

3

THE DETROIT TORPEDO

JIMMY LAVERNE WOULDN'T look me in the eye when I closed the door to his office at the Town Club. It was four o'clock—too early for his business to get under way—and the spot was very quiet. There were a couple of dancers on the floor, and bar trade was pretty slack.

"Sit down," LaVerne told me, sitting down himself. He was pretty uneasy. That was plain to see. Nervously, he picked a cigar out of his pocket and bit off the end. He lighted it before he spoke again. "Well," he asked hesitantly, "did you find him?"

"I found him," I said.

"Did you tell him?"

"I told him," I said. "He's lamming. But he needs cash to do it and he's afraid to risk going to his bank. He wrote out a two grand check to you. Will you cash it?"

"Sure," LaVerne said. His eyes flickered uncertainly and his voice was hushed. I'd never seen him like that. He was one of the whitest props on Broadway, and the Town Club was a gambling spot where the wheels were straight. LaVerne had always given me an impression that he could handle anything. But he sure was bothered then. "Did he talk?"

I nodded. "He was here last night. He overheard you talking to a man from Detroit."

"Eavesdropping?" LaVerne asked.

"Yeah. He thought you had a dame in here and he wanted the item. He still doesn't know who bumped Dunner. No names were mentioned in your talk with the bumper-offer. But I suppose that doesn't make any difference."

LaVerne shook his head. "It doesn't, Daffy. Now listen. I've always been square with you. You've always been square with me. I'm going to tell you something." He took Lyons' check, which I handed to him, and opened his safe as he went on. "You know the code I have. You can bet as much as in my house. No limit on anything. If you win, I pay off. If you lose, you pay off. There's one thing I don't stand for."

"I know," I said. "A welsher."

He nodded, opening a drawer of the safe. "That's right. You remember that Dr. French who tried to welsh? There was an instance. It's a straight gambler's code, Daffy, that a loser pays. We're human guys, we are, and if a boy's in trouble about paying but is really trying to pay, we help him along. But if we find a bird who welshes with no intention of ever paying the debt—"

"I know," I said. "Cocked dice. He's bumped. It's self-protection, Jimmy. It may not be legal, but I guess murder is necessary sometimes." I paused. "If you're trying to tell me that Vinnie Dunner welshed, I know that. Lyons told me what he heard. Dunner was in the hole a hundred grand and took a powder. The bumper-offer followed him from Detroit and wrote off the debt this afternoon."

LaVerne shook his head. "Daffy, Lyons had better watch himself. He's too damn cocky. That's a lot to know—even for you. But that wasn't what I was getting at. I want to tell you why Lyons had better lam."

He handed me the two grand in cash and I counted it to check while he talked. "Me," he went on, "I'm not afraid of anybody in the racket—except this guy from Detroit. He's tough, Daffy. And he'd sooner work a trigger than argue."

"But it's so damn silly!" I said. "Couldn't you talk to him, whoever he is, and let him know that Lyons is just hare-brained?"

"Talk to him?" LaVerne exclaimed. He held out his hand. It was shaking a little. "See that? I'm scared. I'm admitting it to you, Daffy. I'm scared. You know why? Because when Dynamite reads that Lyons' chatter he's going to think. He'll trace it, right back here. He may get an idea that I've double-crossed him myself. I'll have to explain my own position. If he found out that I was helping Lyons take a powder… No, Daffy, I can't talk to him. Hair-trigger guys make me nervous anyhow."

"So the guy from Detroit," I said, "is Dynamite Torkey?"

LaVerne looked startled. "Uh-huh," he said. "Did I give it—"

"I guessed," I said. "You mentioned Dynamite. Torkey is the only big name from Detroit these days. Okay, Jimmy. I guess that's the way it stands. Lyons better take it on the run." I got up. "I don't suppose *I* could talk Torkey out of it?"

LaVerne went white. "Are you crazy, Daffy?"

"I might do the trick."

"Sure you might. You might also get a slug along with Lyons. I'm telling you, Torkey is a mean—"

He stopped and frowned at me. "Are you serious?"

"Sure," I said.

"You realize that if you don't swing it, he'll—"

"Try to kill me, sure." I shrugged. "It wouldn't be the first time I dodged a slug. I guess it wouldn't bother you any if the law caught up with Torkey?"

LaVerne didn't say anything for a minute or so. He sat there, smoking, and he considered me.

"Okay, Daffy," he said finally. "I never told you that he was staying at the Grenada Hotel."

"Thanks," I said, and left.

DYNAMITE TORKEY WAS located on the fourth floor of the Grenada. All the suites look alike anyhow, and I'd been in so many of them there, after various stories for the paper, that his didn't seem one inch out of the way.

But he himself did. When I knocked on the door he called, "Come in."

And when I went in I found him sitting behind a table, facing me alertly, both his hands out of sight under the table.

He had a wide forehead and a narrow chin. His whole face sloped down and in, giving him a wolfish sort of look. His eyes were gray. They didn't shift either. They weren't furtive. They fixed on mine and did a lot of boring, and they had a gleam that took away my good spirits and made me knock knees. He had a big bulb on the end of his nose, too. It had a sheen like ice. There wasn't any expression at all on his face. He said:

"Thought you were the bellboy." His lips didn't even move. "Who are you?"

I kept my hands away from my pockets. "My name's Dill," I said.

He said coldly, "Dill? Never heard of you."

"Joe Dill," I said. "I'm a reporter for the *Chronicle*. My friends call me Daffy."

"What do you want?" he said quickly.

"I want to talk to you," I replied. "I've got something on my mind."

"Sure," he said coldly. "Close the door." I closed it. "Have a seat right there." He nodded to a chair opposite him. I walked over to it and plumped down. "Are you heeled?"

"Naw," I said. "I'm a reporter. On the level. The *Chronicle*."

He took a deep breath and lifted his hands from under the table. He had a pair of .45 Colts in them. They were ugly-looking rods. His face broke and a faint, leering smile curled his lips when he saw me gulp. He put the guns away and lighted a cigarette. "The *Chronicle*, eh? Daffy Dill. Yeah, I *have* heard of you, at that. You caught that jewel-heister, LaSalle."

"I helped."

"Yeah, I read about it in the papers." He flicked his thumb over his shoulder behind him. I saw a copy of the Wall Street Closing edition of the *Chronicle*. "I was just reading your paper when you knocked." It was queer how he spoke. His mouth hardly moved. "Do you know this Harry Lyons?"

I nodded uneasily. "That's what I want to talk to you about."

His face froze. "Yeah?"

"I guess you read that bit about Vinnie Dunner?" I said. "I want to explain."

His eyes looked right into mine. "Go ahead."

"Lyons was at the Town Club last night," I said. "He eavesdropped when a fellow was in talking to Jimmy LaVerne, understand? He heard that Vinnie Dunner might be bumped today. He thought he'd be smart—he's pretty young and cocky—and scoop the rest of us. He printed the tip before it actually happened."

"Keep talking," Dynamite ordered.

"Well, that's all. He didn't hear the name of the bird who was going to do it, and he doesn't know anything else about it. Now he's afraid the guy who did it will come after him, thinking he knows something that may help the police. But he doesn't."

"Yeah?" Torkey said. He relaxed a little. "Why come to me, Dill?"

I shrugged. "Thought you might get that info to the fellow who rubbed out Vinnie."

"What do you know about it?"

"Nothing."

"Yeah? Then how'd you know I was in town? How'd you know where I was staying? How'd you know that I might know the guy who put the slug on Vinnie Dunner?" He sat up straight. "Lay down your cards, Dill. You haven't spilled everything."

"All right!" I exclaimed. "You want a showdown, Dynamite? I'll tell you. I cover the underworld, see? I know that Vinnie Dunner welshed on a gambling debt. I know the gambler's code. A welsher doesn't last long. But I've known a lot of things, Dynamite, that I've forgotten. I've been in the newspaper racket a long time, and I'm still alive. Now this kid, Lyons, is square. He doesn't know a thing. And right now he's sitting in my apartment, terrified, scared to death that you'll catch up with him and machine-gun him like you did Vinnie this afternoon."

Torkey smiled. "Careful, Dill."

"I mean it," I said. "He's about nuts. And if you're a square guy you'll believe me and let him off. He's had his lesson. He doesn't know a thing he could tell the cops."

"But you do," Torkey said.

"Me, I'm different," I said. "Ask Latham of the Hideaway. Ask LaVerne of the Town Club. Ask them all. I play ball and live longer. *If* the other party plays ball too."

"What the hell!" Torkey said suddenly, grinning. "The cops have nothing on me." He relaxed and put out his cigarette. Then he laughed. "No kidding," he said, "is Lyons scared?"

"Delirious," I said.

"That's hot," he said, laughing. "That's pretty hot! Thinks I'd give him the works and take chances with my rap, huh? He must have a lot of gall, that kid!"

I perked up. "Are you on the level? It's okay?"

"SURE IT'S OKAY," Torkey scoffed. "Forget it. I admit I was wondering about Lyons. But if you say it's all right, that settles it. I'm a square guy, Dill. I'll play ball. You beat it home and tell Lyons to save his money instead of spending it on a trip."

I got to my feet and stuck out my hand. We shook. "I knew you were a white man," I said fervently. "Thanks a hell of a lot, Dynamite. If I can do something for you sometime—"

"Sure, sure," he grinned. "I know how it is. Go on now. Beat it home and tell Lyons before he has a stroke." He didn't look at me when he spoke, but he slapped me on the back. I waved good-by to him and went out.

When I got out of the elevator down in the resplendent lobby of the Grenada I lighted a cigarette, feeling pretty good, and I started out for the revolving door.

I had to pass the telephone boards on the way. I saw Gertie Dodge, a hard-boiled little gal who often tipped me off to news at the Grenada. I called, "Hi, Gert!" and waved.

"Daffy!" she said. "Com'ere and see a friend."

I grinned at her and went over. "You look pretty good," she said. "Haven't seen you for a month. Where you heading? Up to see our prize catch—Dynamite Torkey?"

"Just saw him," I said. "I'm on my way home."

"You just—"

She scowled at me. "You just saw him? Now that's queer, damned queer."

"Why?"

"Why? He just put a call through my switchboard to your newspaper. He asked them for your home address."

I dropped my cigarette on the floor and stamped on it. "What did you say?"

"You heard me! He asked for your home address, and, what's more, he got it!"

It came to me. That's why he hadn't looked me in the eye when he said it was all okay. That's why he changed so quickly and slapped my back. He was waiting for me to get home and tell Lyons that everything was cleaned up.

And then he was going to arrive right after me and rub out the both of us!

"Daffy!" Gert exclaimed, watching my face. "What is it?"

"A double-cross!" I said. "Stand by, Gert, and thanks for my life!"

4

THE KILLER'S TAXI

I TOOK THE third booth in line beyond the switchboards and put through a quick call to my own apartment. From where I stood I had a plain view of the elevator bank, and I wasn't planning to miss a thing. In a few seconds Lyons answered.

"Hello?" he said in a tight voice, and for once I couldn't blame him. My own pipes were pretty clogged.

I said, "Harry, this is Daffy. Now get me straight and don't lose your head, understand?"

"Go ahead," he croaked. "I can take it, I guess."

"Things have gone wrong," I said. "Your bumper-offer is Dynamite Torkey of Detroit. I saw him and tried to talk him out of any idea he had concerning you. He said okay, but he's planning a double-cross. He's going to head for my place with the intention of killing both of us. I'm in it now as much as you; more so, in fact. He knows that I know that he killed Dunner. Not so good."

Lyons asked shakily, "What're we going to do, Daffy?"

"You sit tight," I said. "Lock and bar the door. I'm going to tail him over myself. And I'm calling Poppa Hanley at h.q. and asking for help. I don't know what we'll do, but if you lock the door he can't get in. And remember—in case he should—there's a fire escape in my bedroom that goes up to the roof. But don't leave the apartment if you can help it, get me? We've got to get a charge against this bird to put him in the can. Otherwise he'll go out on the loose again and only try some other time. Got all that?"

"Yeah," Lyons said in a choked voice. "I'll stick, Daffy."

I hung up. Fishing another nickel out of my jeans, I dropped it in the coin box and was about to ask for my number when one of the doors at the elevator bank opened. I stiffened.

Torkey walked out of it slowly. Under his arm he was carrying a violin case.

"Hi-ho!" I muttered and got the hell out of the booth as fast as I could.

I stopped by Gertie Dodge and snapped:

"Gert, pal, get this and get it straight or you'll weep at my funeral. Torkey just came out of the elevator. When he passes you, call him over and stall him for at least a minute. Tell him some one called him or something—*but stall him!* When he leaves, call Bill Hanley at the homicide bureau and tell him to come in person at the head of a flying squad. My place. Tell him the Vinnie Dunner killer is after Dill. He'll know. Check?"

"Double-check," Gert nodded. "Scram!"

I went through the revolving door out onto the sidewalk. There was a line of cabs at the curb. The driver of the first called, "Taxi?"

I ran around the side of the cab. I said:

"Fifty bucks for a loan of your cap and your hack, Mac. I'm Daffy Dill of the *Chronicle* and I need both bad. Yes or no?"

"Fifty fish!" he exclaimed. "Will you bring it back?"

"In an hour," I said. "Right back here."

"I'll say," the driver replied, hopping out. "Pass me the fifty, pal. Here's the cap. There is a Santa Claus after all these years?"

I handed him a fifty-fish bill which I yanked from the roll which Jimmy LaVerne had given to me when he cashed Harry Lyons' check. Then I shed my own hat and coat and threw them at the driver. "Hang onto these until I bring back the hack," I said. "I'll see you later."

Tilting his cap on the side of my head, I climbed up into the front seat of the cab. I wasn't any too quick, either. I'd hardly settled myself when Dynamite Torkey came out of the hotel through the revolving door. I watched him. His lean face was sallow in the daylight and lined like a topographical map. It was just as inscrutable as one also. He glanced cautiously up and down the avenue. When passers-by were sparse, he stepped towards the curb and raised his hand.

I shifted and pulled the hack up under the Grenada's swanky canopy. He opened the back door without looking at me. As a matter of fact, he hid his face so that I couldn't see it. A canny gent, thought I. Doesn't want a cabby to identify him later. He sat down in back.

"Where to, sir?" I asked gruffly.

"Never mind, driver," he said. "Just coast. I'll tell you later." He was being canny again. Didn't want any chance eavesdropper to get the destination. I stepped on the gas and moved out into traffic. Only then did he tell me. "Madison Avenue and Forty-fifth Street," he said. "And step on it."

The hack had what it takes. It jumped ahead nicely when I gave it the gun. I turned and headed down Park Avenue, the lights all with me. At Forty-fifth Street I turned right and went across on the one-way street. The red lights held me up at Lexington Avenue. I glanced in the rear vision mirror. Torkey was sitting all slumped down on the leather cushions. His face was still covered and he appeared to be glancing out of the window at his right. His violin case he held in his left arm, resting the base on the seat.

The lights changed to green. I shifted and rode the hack hard to the corner of Madison Avenue. I heard him call, "Right here, driver. I'll get off right here."

I pulled up at the curb and started to turn when a one-spot was thrust through the window at me. "Keep the change," he said.

"Thanks," I said. I shifted and turned left down Madison Avenue. In the rear vision mirror I saw him cross Madison and walk down Forty-fifth towards Fifth Avenue. My apartment was midway in that block. Now was the time for all good men to come to the aid of their prey! I yanked the hack into the first parking space I could find, shut off the engine and got out.

TORKEY HAD DISAPPEARED from view. I ran like hell back up Madison to Forty-fifth and peered around the corner. There he was, just going up the stone steps of Number 67, my spot being on the top floor of the house. My hands were shaking pretty badly. When he had entered I crossed to the other side of the street until I reached a point directly opposite my own doorway. Here I stopped and lighted a cigarette.

There was no sign of Poppa Hanley and his squad car

of riot men. There was no distant sound of the siren of his crate either. The street was rather still, except for the rumbling of a bus on Fifth Avenue, and the occasional *beep-beep* of a hack on Madison.

I watched my bedroom. It was four flights up on the front of the house. The top fire escape platform was just outside the two bedroom windows. From it, up to the roof, a narrow steel ladder ascended. This was what I had warned Lyons about.

Nothing happened....

"Poppa, Poppa!" I muttered. "For God's sake, come along before Torkey leaves with his violin!" I puffed furiously on my cig until the smoke stung my lungs, and I scanned the street for some sign of the squad car. There was none.

Without warning, I heard a strange muffled chatter as of some one rattling a pair of sticks across a drum. Then the sudden squeak of a window thrown open, followed by a wild yell.

I stared up at my bedroom. There was Harry Lyons climbing out of the bedroom window and bellowing, "Murder! Murder!" at the top of his lungs!

I was struck dumb. I couldn't move. All I could hear was Harry's cries and the thumping of my own heart. I watched him climb up the steel ladder to the roof. He'd no sooner disappeared over the parapet than Torkey leaped out onto the fire escape from the bedroom and went up the ladder to the roof also, his sub-machine gun dangling in his left hand.

That shoved me off. I went across that street and into the vestibule like an arrow. Up the stairs three at a time.

I was so excited I never even felt the strain on my legs. I reached the top floor in one minute flat, and I flung into my own rooms.

Up above me, through the open window, I heard the machine-gun stutter sharply a few times!

I tore open my desk. In the top drawer lay my very own .32 Colt, a small gun which I had bought for emergencies, but which I did not usually carry. I flipped open the chamber, saw it fully loaded. At the same time I started for the bedroom.

As I dove through the open window onto the fire escape a shrill wailing of a siren filled the street. I looked down below me and saw a black police car jerk up to the curb, tires squealing under the pressure of the abrupt stop. Men piled out. Poppa Hanley was among the first. I could make out his broad shoulders and long nose. I roared: *"Poppa!"*

He twitched, startled, and looked up.

"On the roof!" I yelled as the machine gun started to hammer again. "He's here on the roof! *Hurry up!*"

Hanley ran into the house. I gripped the .32 and went up the ladder, feeling pretty dizzy from the height. Poking my head over the edge of the parapet carefully, I took in the whole lay.

Torkey was standing in the open center of the roof, moving slowly to the left so that he could spot Harry, who had taken protection behind the raised brick uprights of the roof door. It wasn't much protection, either; because by feinting Torkey could maneuver Harry out on the other side of the door into range. Each time that he'd feint Torkey would let go a round of slugs at Lyons.

As I stared, the whole setup got Lyons' nerves. He tore

from behind the door and tried to get around so that he could break through the door and run down the stairs. He was white as a ghost—whiter, maybe—and I never saw such horrible terror in a man's eyes before. Torkey spotted him as he ran and swung the Tommy gun around from his hip as he pressed the trigger.

The gun jumped as it chattered, and slugs spouted tar where they hit the roofing. They went across in a curved line, kicking up dirt and roofing not less than three feet behind Lyons' churning legs. One little swing further would do the trick.

I slammed my own gun over the edge of the parapet and fired at Torkey twice, holding onto the steel ladder with my left hand. The .32 cracked sharp, high and clear and quite distinct above the chatter of the machine gun. It was a shot by instinct. I just fired in his general direction. I couldn't aim, hanging onto that ladder about a hundred and fifty feet above some very hard cement pavement. Naturally I missed.

But I didn't miss much. The slugs kicked up tar splinters about a foot behind Torkey. He must have heard the shots and then sensed the impact of the slugs. He stopped firing at Lyons and wheeled around like a trapped rat, the Tommy gun still swinging from his hip.

BEHIND HIM, I saw Lyons make the roof door and dive down the stairs. Then Torkey held the black nozzle of the machine gun on my skull and pressed the trigger.

I was down below the parapet before the first burst clattered. But his aim gave me icy shivers. The wad of slugs grated whiningly against the stone edge of the parapet where my young blue eyes had been and then zoomed off into space to smack solidly against the brick walls of the building across the street, raining chips down into the street.

Keeping my head low, I gauged about where Torkey would be standing up above me on the roof, and I stuck my fist over the parapet and fired twice more at him.

The machine gun stopped firing and I heard him curse harshly. Taking advantage of the respite, I stuck my head over the parapet, took a pretty quick bead on him and fired my fifth shot.

I caught him through the left arm, and he dropped the machine gun with a groan of pain and fury.

Starting to climb over the edge of the parapet, I saw him dive for the machine gun again, pick it up with his right hand, raise it and fire at me. Down I went on the ladder again as the bullets danced over my head. They stopped suddenly. I took off the taxi driver's hat and stuck it on the end of my gun barrel. I held it up.

Wham! The hat was torn off the barrel and flew down into the street in shreds. Enough bullets hit it for me to start a munitions factory of my own. Torkey had waited for my head. And he'd gotten my hat instead. But I figured he still thought my head had been in the hat.

With one slug left in my gun, I jumped down to the fire escape and climbed back into my apartment. Torkey had to pass my door to get downstairs and lam. I went through to the front door just as I heard the roof door slam over my head.

Only then did I see how Torkey had gotten into the place. The door jamb was shot away, as was the lock, and

there were raw scars in the wood where the slugs had
served as a key.

There was thudding on the staircase from the roof. I
pressed myself back behind the wall of my apartment and
waited. Torkey came by my door so fast that he had reached
the next descending level of the stairs before I got out into
the open.

His machine gun was gone. In his right hand he was
holding one of those ugly .45s which he had had in the
hotel room. I don't know why, but when he started down
to the third floor I let out a yell and, instead of taking good
aim, I flung a wild shot at him which banged the wall over
his head.

He wheeled around, surprised, his mouth set, his teeth
gleaming like an animal's. Wrapping my fist around my
empty gun as though it were a baseball, I heaved it at him
with all my strength just as he threw a quick shot from the
.45 at me.

I missed his head, but the gun bounced off his wounded
arm, and the pain jerked him around so that his bullet only
combed my hair, without parting it.

He must have thought he had gotten me, for he started
down the stairs again out of my sight. I heard him grunt
once or twice and then I heard the .45 roar again. It was
instantly followed by the grim clatter of a machine gun.

I reached the banister and leaned over, looking down. I
was just in time to see Torkey—bent double, his head down
towards his knees—topple head over heels down the rest
of the stairs to the third floor, rolling like a ball.

He hit the landing with a crash, banging up against
the banister there and cracking it. Then he unfolded as

he stretched out prone. I didn't need any sawbones to tell me that he was dead. His whole belly was studded with little black holes, just like Vinnie Dunner's. Like Vinnie Dunner, he would not be eating supper that night, either.

While I was staring down below, a homely pan peered around the edge of the staircase on the third floor, took a good look at the still corpse on the landing, and then glanced up at me. It was Poppa Hanley, with a police machine gun in his paws. He saw me and grinned.

He said:

"Come out, come out, wherever you are!" in a sing-song like the kids use when they play cops and robbers.

"Poppa!" I called. "Is Harry Lyons all right?"

"Yeah," Hanley said. "The boys are taking care of him downstairs. He's got pink elephants on his shoulder, he's that scared. Come on down."

"In a minute," I said. I went back into the apartment and called the Old Man. He gave me Brad for rewrite and I spilled the whole yarn. The Old Man listened in on it, and when I got through he was laughing so hard I thought he'd choke. "Daffy," he said, "you're killing me. The whole thing really happened to Harry Lyons, and now that it's all over you're scooping him on his own story!"

"Ain't it so," I murmured and I hung up. It was a pleasant thought and it made me feel better when I went downstairs to the street. I found Harry in the squad car, still jittery. I gave him his roll.

"I had to spend fifty to hire a hack in order to tail Torkey," I said. "You're alive and well, so you should kick."

He couldn't speak. He just nodded dumbly. Hanley came over. "I have to wait for the M.E. to check on the stiff

before we cart him to the morgue, Daffy. You go down with
the boys in the squad car if you want to. Halloran will want
your testimony down for the inquest."

"Nerts," I said. "I'll see him tomorrow. First I've got to
take a taxicab back to its owner."

"Well," he said, "can't you come down to h.q. after that?"

I sighed and shook my head. "My fran," I said emphat-
ically, "I have a very important engagement after that. It is
an engagement I should have kept at one o'clock. Shorty
McGinnis made the date for me. And now—if you will
pardon me—I'll keep that date once and for all."

Hanley grinned. "Sure," he said. "Who's it with?"

"An Old-fashioned," I replied, "waiting for me lone-
somely at this moment behind the Hideaway Club bar."

And—as Shorty had told me—it was the tastiest charge
I ever guzzled anywhere on the main stem.

THE DANCING CORPSE

*The Red-Headed Ghost That Walked
Forty-Fourth Street by Daylight and
Danced the Rhumba at Night Hands
Daffy Dill a Double Riddle*

1

THE GHOST ON FORTY-FOURTH STREET

HARRY LYONS WAS sick. The New York *Chronicle*, which hands me forty-five shekels a week for slaving away my young life in quest of news, was without a daily chatter colyum. So when the Old Man called me into his private doghouse on the far side of the city room and politely asked me to substitute on Harry's colyum I said, "Why not?"

"I'm asking *you*," said the Old Man mildly sarcastic. "Will you cover for him or not?"

"Magnanimous me," I said with an angelic smile. "The shirt off my back for a pal. Sure I'll cover."

"A pal?" The Old Man pushed up his green eyeshade and made a distinctly unpleasant sound not unlike several ripe raspberries. "How times have changed! Or have you forgotten the day when he got you canned for that libel you wrote about the chef of the Waldorf Towers?"

I said darkly, "A Dill never forgets."

"Neither do elephants," replied the Old Man. "Then why the sudden brotherly love?"

"Ah, well," I said. "Who am I to hold a grudge? Besides, I am broke and badly bent. It occurred to me that a tour of the Gay White Way would not be bad at all. Especially when this imitation of a newspaper is paying the expense of my delicious debauchery."

"I see," the Old Man leered. "Anything for a pal! Okay, Daffy. On your way. And for God's sake, put a little news in that colyum. Harry has been padding it. Everything I read in it sounds stale."

"No wonder," I said. "He clips Winston's colyum in the *Globe.*"

The Old Man looked at me sourly. "Never mind that. You bring back some fresh news. That colyum is a swell spot for hot flashes. I know you won't clip Winston's stuff because you can't read English. And don't get goo-goo-eyed staring at the frail damsels tonight. Business first, last and always—and no pleasure."

"Business," I said with dignity, "it shall be. To-night at eleven o'clock, Daffy Dill will soar out on the Dawn Patrol—and I won't come back 'til it's over over there!"

"Plagiarist," growled the Old Man.

"Now scram and let me work."

I left him alone, hoping he might bite himself in the throat and give himself hydrophobia thereby. I went through the city room to the outer offices of the *Chronicle,* where a platinum-haired thing of beauty was sitting behind a small desk, directing sundry corpulent gents in the direction of the classified ad department. This gel was Dinah Mason, who gives me goose-pimples and a bad case of marital heartache. I sauntered over to her nonchalantly, tweeked her right ear and said, "Hello, Angel-Eyes!"

"Hello, Rasputin," she said. "And that's *my* ear. What do you want from me?"

I heard the squeak of my apartment door opening

"Marriage," I said, "and no wise-cracks. Today's proposal makes the ninety-eighth. Will you marry me?"

"Ha-ha," she said gloomily.

"Then I take it," I said, "that the answer is no?"

"As ever. Now evacuate so's we poletariat can breathe something besides hot air."

"Hokey, hokey," I snapped, "but recall, my friend, that I promised you exactly one hundred proposals. You have two chances left to accept me. After that I will commit suicide."

"Tsk tsk," she said.

I went through the door in tragedy so deep it would have put Hamlet to shame. When I reached the street and realized that Dinah wasn't an audience any more, the tragedy left me abruptly and I considered my ways and means. I had a fin in my jeans and nothing to do until nightfall. Seeing as how summer was just left behind, it seemed appropriate that I should warm my innards with the delectable constituents of an Old-Fashioned.

I took the Eighth Avenue subway uptown to Forty-Second Street and Times Square, and walked up Broadway until I came to the green and white canopy of the Hideaway Club, Bill Latham's popular rendezvous for the not-so-tired business man. Early afternoon meant that the place would be empty, and when I went in I found it practically deserted. Bill Latham himself was standing at the bar talking with Shorty McGinnis, who hurls the alkie to and fro for the paying customers.

I said, "Salutations, friends, and one Old-Fashioned."

Shorty grinned and went to work on the drink while Bill Latham hit me on the back in his inimitable way and exclaimed, "And where in hell have you been for the last three days?"

"Out and around," I said. "What's new?"

"Nothing," Latham said.

"I'm covering the Dawn Patrol to-night," I said. "It develops that Harry Lyons is flat on his back. They say it's the grippe, but I'll bet he's got a swell case of *mal-de-mer* induced by fear of the bumper-offer who was after him."

"Here's your drink, Daffy," Shorty said, pushing it over the bar.

"Thanks, friend," I chirped. I lifted it triumphantly for the first delicious inhale—when suddenly the swinging doors of the Hideaway burst open with a crash like summer thunder and a guy plunged through them like a ram.

"Hey—!" Bill Latham started to protest. But he didn't get a chance to finish. The guy tore across the room to the bar, where he pulled up right beside me, panting and heaving. When he could speak he waved at Shorty and croaked:

"Whisky straight! No water!"

HE WAS A little guy, about five feet five, dressed in a flashy suit and sporting a black bowler. He had a nose like a hot dog, and when he reached out for the liquor I could see that he had had a bad shock. His skin was waxy, absolutely drained of all blood. Under his eyes, in distinct bags, the flesh was nearly black. I thought he was going to faint. In his left hand he was holding a morning paper. He threw off a jigger, and then filled it again.

I nudged Bill Latham and whispered, "Who is he?"

"Benny the Shill," Latham said. "You know, Benny Cassell, the actor's press agent?"

"Looks like a yarn," I said. "Make him give."

"Hello, Benny," Latham called. "What's the matter?"

Cassell waved a limp hand at Latham and finished the second jigger of rye. He made an awful face, but he got it down and kept it down. He took a deep breath finally and gasped, "My God! Such things can't be!"

"Take it easy," said Latham, frowning. "You look as though you'd seen a ghost."

"*A ghost!*" Cassell cried. "That's it! You hit the nail on the head! That's what I have seen! A ghost on Forty-Fourth Street I saw—"

I cautioned, "Hey, friend, slow down. You'll ruin your pipes. What is this hocus-pocus about a ghost?"

He eyed me suspiciously and poured out a third jigger. He turned to Bill and flicked his thumb over his shoulder at me. "Who's this guy?"

"Daffy Dill," Latham said. "You know. The news-hound."

Immediately, the suspicion went out of Benny Cassell's eyes and he warmed to me. You have to be an ornament of the press to realize how press agents love anything or anybody connected with the Fourth Estate. He figured I was good for his business, and he opened up. "Honest to Moses," he said, speaking like a streamliner, "I just saw a spook on Broadway and Forty-Fourth, and that's no kid!" His voice was husky with sincerity. He was on the level.

I asked, "How come?"

"I was coming down from the theater where my offices are," he replied quickly. "I was just crossing the street at Forty-Fourth when I bumped into this doll. She was a looker all right. I started to give her the go-by when I caught a shot of her pan square on. My God, what a shock! She took one look at me, recognized me, and ran like hell! I took one look at her and ran the opposite way. I never saw such a—"

"Whoa," I said. "Make sense. Did you know her?"

Benny Cassell took a deep breath. "I managed her business connections for eight years," he said. "I ought to know her."

"Then who was she?"

"Dollie Merritt! So help me—it was Dollie Merritt! In the flesh! She had red hair instead of her usual blonde, but that didn't fool me. She knew me, too! She was scared stiff of me!"

Bill Latham was staring at him. It was all too much for me. "Listen," I said dryly, "maybe I'm an ignoramus, but just who is Dollie Merritt, and why should the sight of her scare the pants off you?"

He gaped at me, hoarsely whispering:

"You—don't—know?"

"I don't know," I said. "Spill!"

Slowly shaking his head, he put his newspaper on the bar and spread it out. It was a late city edition of the *Globe,* and he had opened it to the first page of the second section, where the obituaries were listed. I saw a pencil ring around a short news story. Benny Cassell put his finger on it. It went:

DOLLIE MERRITT DIES

Dollie Merritt, prominent for many years in many of Broadway's musical comedies, died yesterday at her apartment in Beauchamp Gardens, Central Park West, of pneumonia induced through ptomaine poisoning. She had been ill of poisoning for a week and her condition so weakened her that hyperstatic broncho-pneumonia set in. On the stage for ten years, she appeared in *Top Speed, Five O'clock Girl, Good News, Hold Everything,* and many other plays. She is survived by an ex-husband, Ronald Fortney, of Denver, Colo.

"Well, well," I said. "I never heard of her, and I saw every one of those shows."

"She wasn't a star," said Latham. "That write-up is just some of Benny's handiwork. She wasn't anything but a bum hoofer. Her dancing wasn't bad at all," he added as Cassell started to protest, "but her disposition and rep smelled to heaven. Blackmail was her best bet. That's really how she made her living. She only danced when she was broke."

"I see," I said. "Well, Benny, if she's dead, you didn't see her today."

"Are you telling me?" Benny Cassell replied grimly.

"Listen, Dill. I was at her bedside when she kicked in. I was right there, see? I saw her die, see? And I'm telling you just the same—I saw Dollie Merritt on Broadway not fifteen minutes ago—alive and well!" He wiped the sweat from his face.

I FINISHED MY Old-Fashioned slowly and considered the little gink. His face was still white and his hands still trembled. He was dead on the level. You can't fake a shock, because it shows in the eyes. He began to get me. None of his story made any sense—and that was a sure sign that there was something in it. I began to get hunches. I put my empty glass on the bar and said do him:

"She's dead. You saw her die. That was yesterday, right?"

"Right!"

"She's alive. You saw her walking. That was today, right?"

"Right, so help me!"

"Yesterday on her death bed, Dollie Merritt was a blonde. To-day, alive and well, Dollie Merritt was a red-head?"

"Yeah." Benny Cassell licked his lips. "Dill—this is straight. No stunt. I don't give a damn what you do about it. I just had to tell somebody, that's all. But if I had to take my pick between the two I'd say it was Dollie I saw today, not yesterday. God, it hit me hard when I saw her—"

"Skip it," I said. "What do you think, Bill?"

Latham smiled thinly. "I think he's hopped to the ears. Dollie Merritt is dead as hell. You can prove that by getting a death transcript from the Board of Health. The only way there could be two Dollie Merritts would be for the stiff to have a twin. Did she, Benny?"

Benny Cassell shook his head. "She was the only one."

"Then," said Latham, "the idea is wet. Furthermore—why such a gag?"

I said, "Now, Billy-boy, is when you get interesting. Suppose Dollie Merritt is really alive, not dead. Why such a gag? And there is the catch. Benny, my fran, you fascinate me, and so to ease my curious brain, how about coming along with me and taking a glam at the corpse… Where is it?"

Benny Cassell choked. "You won't identify her that way. She was cremated this morning at Ferncliff."

I whistled and glanced at Latham. "Died yesterday. Cremated today. Pretty quick work. And expensive, too. Who handled the cost of the thing—her husband, maybe?"

"Her *ex*-husband," Benny corrected. "And he didn't. At least he couldn't have. He's a ham out in Hollywood, trying to get a job. He's broke. He always used to write to her for money." The press agent scowled. "Now that's a funny thing… Who did pay for the cremation? I never thought of that. Dollie didn't have a dime herself. She owed rent on her apartment. And she didn't have no folks."

"We're getting warm," I said, slapping forty cents on the bar in payment for my drink. "Benny, can you get a picture of that dame?"

"Sure. I've got lots of 'em!"

"Hokey. Then you get that picture. And then you phone the undertakers who handled the cremation—know who they were?"

"Yeah, Blackwell's on Sixty-Sixth."

"Ask them who pays the bill. Got that? And then you lam down to the Bureau of Vital Statistics at Centre Street and meet me there. No. Change that. Meet me in the homicide bureau office. That should be in half an hour. Now blow."

He blew. I started out myself, but Bill Latham grabbed my arm.

"Don't be a sap, Daffy. This is no yarn. He's just been seeing things. What in hell will you do down there?"

"Get a death transcript," I replied, "and it should prove very interesting. Yea, verily, William, I shall see you tonight on the Dawn Patrol, and don't take any wooden nickels!"

2

THE RECORD

I WAITED A solid hour while they made up a photostatic copy of the death certificate. And it cost me four bits at that. At three o'clock they finally handed it over to me and I read it.

It was very disappointing. It listed the cause of death of one Dollie Merritt and it was signed by the attending medico, Dr. Howard Planey, of Stanley Place, City. Since there was nothing accidental about the death, the M.E.'s office had not been called in at all. The thing was a closed book. Even if someone made a fuss, you couldn't exhume ashes very well. She'd been sick for exactly eight days.

I folded the thing and put it away, and I went down to the homicide bureau office, where I had promised to meet Benny Cassell.

Lieutenant Bill Hanley was working on some reports in his office when I went in. I said, "Hi, Poppa!"

He groaned. "Just when everything is going along so nice, you show up. What now?"

"It's about a gel named Merritt," I said. "She died yesterday."

Hanley nodded. "I know. Read it in this morning's paper."

"Yeah," I said. "Her press agent says he saw her today. I wondered if he possibly could be right. Did Dollie have a record down here?"

Hanley ogled at me. "What is this stuff? About the walking corpse, I mean."

"Poppa, the press agent was on the level. Maybe he's screwy. Maybe he's got a scoop. I'm trying to find out, The death transcript is all in order, but that doesn't mean anything. If the medico—Planey is his name—were in on a deal, he could write the death certificate and get away with it. He could put Dollie down for dead even if she were alive."

"Nope," Hanley smiled. "There has to be a corpse."

"Granted. The crack still goes."

"Listen, derp," said Hanley. "You can't get away with that sort of stuff in this burg. Friends and relatives would identify the body in the undertaking parlors."

"Granted again. That was done. Her own press agent saw her die. He'd known her for eight years."

Hanley scowled. "The same guy who saw her die saw her alive today?"

"Right, Poppa."

"Then he's nuts."

"Ah," I heckled, "that's only a theory. Where's your evidence? Anyway, let's go look up the numbers on Dollie Merritt. And, by the way—hasn't Benny Cassell showed up here yet?"

"No," said Hanley. "Is he the agent you meant?"

I nodded. "Why?"

Hanley shrugged. "He happens to be a square shooter. Maybe there is something to it. But, hell—corpses don't stroll the avenue the day after death. Isn't Merritt's body somewhere?"

"Sure. In the ozone. Burned this morning at Ferncliff. How you like them berries, fran?"

Hanley frowned. "Let's see the record—"

We went into the fingerprint files of the police department and looked for a card among the M's. We found what we wanted, a record of one Dollie Merritt. Poppa Hanley grunted, mildly surprised. I grabbed the card.

It went something like this: *Robbery—suspended sentence. Violation Sullivan Law—suspended sentence. Blackmail— charges dropped. Indecency-convicted. Blackmail—suspended sentence.*

"Poor Dollie," I sighed. "She was such a sweet goil!"

"When you've finished making faces," Hanley said, "I'll put that card back and return to work."

"Nix, nix. I'm declaring you in. My trouble is your trouble from now on."

Hanley looked bored. "What are you going to do? What do you think has happened? And a lot of other questions...."

I said, "First, I think there's been a murder. Second, I think there is a shakedown. Third, I think, maybe, there is a swindle on the make. Fourth, I'm sure Dollie Merritt is as dead as your left foot."

"My left foot ain't dead."

"That's the point."

WHEN WE GOT back to his office, Benny Cassell hadn't arrived. I looked at Hanley's desk clock and saw that it was an hour and a half since I'd left the little agent at the Hideaway Club. I didn't like it, because I began to have funny hunches. I sat down with Poppa to wait for Benny and I asked, "Ever hear of a Dr. Ralph Planey? He lives in Stanley Place, uptown."

"Planey, Planey…" Hanley muttered. "Yeah, that's familiar, Daffy. Seems to me that Shane and his vice squad had a run-in with a medico named Planey."

I asked, "What for?"

"Not reporting gunshot wounds. Sawbones for a mob."

"We're getting hot," I said. "Hot indeed. If it's the same Planey, he wouldn't hesitate to make—" I stopped and looked at the clock and scowled.

"Now what?" Hanley asked.

"It's Cassell," I said. "I told him to meet me here. That was more than an hour ago. I'm worried about him."

"Why?"

"Listen, idiot, don't you see? Suppose Planey and Dollie Merritt were pulling a racket. Suppose some one else died and Planey signed a death certificate for Dollie Merritt. Then, today, Benny Cassell sees Dollie after she is supposed to be dead. He recognizes her. That recognition means that he is a threat to the plan, whatever it is. That would put him in danger, in case—"

The telephone on Poppa Hanley's desk rang. I stopped speaking while he picked up the handset and said:

"Hello? Homicide bureau." There was a short pause and he glanced up at me, smothering the mouthpiece as he whispered, "Stick around. Call coming through the telegraph bureau." He listened a moment, then said, "Yeah, yeah, Hanley on the wire. Give it to me." He listened some more and made notes on a small pad beside his right hand.

I read the notes over his shoulder as he scribbled them.

His face got grimmer as the call persisted and the written words went:

> *Homicide at Room 1447 Rothy Building, Fiftieth Street and Broadway. Man about thirty-five years old stabbed in back with bronze letter opener. Body found by a Jane Fisher, who identified it as Benny Cassell, press agent.*

"Thanks," Hanley said. He hung up and dropped the pencil on the desk, staring moodily at the pad. Finally he raised his gray eyes to meet my own. "Guess Benny won't keep that date with you."

"Looks like he won't," I said. My ticker was turning over plenty revolutions per second and I felt queer. Hate began to bud in me, hate for the whole rotten mysterious business that had snuffed out Benny Cassell's life. I clenched my fists tightly.

Hanley noticed it and sighed. "Easy does it," he said. He got to his feet and pulled out his .38 and inspected the cylinder to make sure it was primed for action. "Sometimes, Daffy, I think you and your hunches are plain batty, but in the end things never are as screwloose as they seem. I'm with you all the way. Dollie Merritt ain't any more dead than I am. And it begins to look like we've run into a honey of a case. Suppose we take a run uptown and glam the stiff."

"Suppose we do," I said shortly. I was thinking of a little guy, pale and excited, drinking jiggers of rye and babbling about a walking spook. Now he was stretched out cold and he-wouldn't do any more jigger-filling. He wouldn't do any more ghost-seeing, either. And he wouldn't do any identifying of the dame with the red hair....

We left Poppa Hanley's office and went uptown.

3

THE NAME ON THE BLOTTER

BENNY CASSELL'S OFFICE was on the fifth floor of the Rothy Building. It wasn't much. The floor was filled with small private offices, each of them about ten feet square. In the outer foyer of the floor itself there was a main switchboard which handled all the calls for all of the offices. This Jane Fisher, a little brunette who found the corpse and who kept her head despite the gruesomeness of the situation, was the doll who handled the switchboard.

There were a couple of flat feet in the office and a fingerprint man from the 47th precinct. Jane Fisher was standing in the outer hall, away from the death office. She was white and shaken, but still holding on. Hanley nudged me and went right into the office. I didn't follow him.

Instead, I parked beside the girl for a minute. "You found him?" I said.

She nodded.

"How come?"

"I was at the switchboard," she replied weakly. "An outgoing call came from his office. I plugged in and someone in his office asked me if I would run downstairs a minute and get some spirits of ammonia for Mr. Cassell, as he had fainted. I ran right down, and when I came up again and went in—there he was—on the floor—"

"Skip that part," I said, "and squattez-vous in this chair. Now listen, lady. Could you identify the voice you heard on the phone?"

Jane Fisher looked blank. "No. It was all muffled and sounded funny. I'm sure it was disguised."

"Sure," I said. "How long were you downstairs?"

"Not more than five minutes."

"Were you at your switchboard all the time before that?"

"No," she answered quickly. "I'd only been back from lunch about fifteen minutes. Mr. Cassell came in after I had come in."

I looked surprised. I got up and went over to her switchboard and sat down in her chair. The spot commanded a view of the door to Benny Cassell's office. "Lady, lady," I said, "let me get this straight. You went out to lunch. A few minutes after you got back, Benny Cassell came in, right?" She nodded. "Hokey. Then who came into his office after that?"

She said, "No one, honestly. No one did "

"But," I said, "Benny Cassell was not the one who asked you to go downstairs for a minute."

"That's right," she said, her hands plucking at her dress nervously, "Then the man must have gone in while I was out to lunch!"

I smiled. "Hunky-dory. So it was a man. And what time were you out to lunch?"

"One to one-thirty. I know that for sure. I do it every day."

"Good." I got up and pressed the elevator buzzer. There

was a short wait while the arrow over the doors showed that the cage was on its way up. Suddenly the doors clanged open.

"Going down!"

"Going nowhere, my friend," I told the elevator man. "Step forth from yon chariot a second and riddle me this: Between one and one-thirty, did you bring a man up to the fifth floor?"

The elevator man shook his head. "Naw. The cops asked me that one already. I told them the only guy I took up during that time was a gazabo who went to the eighth."

"Could you—" I began.

"No," he snapped. "I couldn't. I don't look over all the mugs I ride up and down. I've gotta enough to think about without playing detective all over the place. I don't even know whether he was a white man. Now lay off and don't bother me again." The doors slammed and he disappeared.

Jane Fisher sighed. "I'll bet the man who went to the eighth was the one who did it!" she said. "He could have gone up there to avert suspicion, walked down three flights to the fifth, seen that no one was at the switchboard and gone into the office to wait for Mr. Cassell. Then when he called me, I left, and he killed Mr. Cassell and made a getaway before I returned."

"You're too smart for your own good, lady," I said soberly. "If you want to make theories, make 'em. But keep 'em to yourself or you'll find yourself in the morgue some bright and cheerful morning. That last resume was too bull's-eye for longevity."

I tipped the hat and left her for the private office. Bill Hanley was leaning over the prone figure on the floor. He glanced up at me when I came in. One of the cops tried to keep me out, but Hanley said, "Nix, nix. He stays."

I said, "So what, Poppa, so what?"

"Neat job," said Hanley. "Caught him right through the left lung and must have impaled his pump. These birds called the M.E., so I expect he's on his way up. I don't need that buzzard to tell me this gink is dead."

Cassell's face was at right angles with the ceiling. It was a waxy white, the lips as snowy as the skin, the eyes wide open, with the relaxed muscles of the irises making them big black pools, sightless and awful. I sighed. "Hi-ho, Poppa, I never did see a stiff yet who looked pleasant. What've you found?"

POPPA HANLEY LOOKED pleased with himself. He reached over to Benny's desk and picked up something in a white handkerchief. Unfolding the handkerchief, he showed the object to be a letter-opener. It was a gem of a weapon—heavy, smooth-handled, sharp-knifed.

I sighed. "I suppose the killer left his name and address and a signed confession on the desk?"

"It amounts to the same thing," Hanley said. "Take a glam at this sweet little tip." He held the heavy handle of the letter-opener over toward me. Apparently, the finger-print man from the 47th had been at work on the thing with his gray print powder. Way down on the handle, right next to the blade itself, a single fingerprint stood out like a front page streamer.

I ogled. "How come, Poppa?"

"It's a pinkey print," Hanley said. "That right, Guilfoyle?"

The dick from the 47th nodded. "Fifth finger of the right hand," he grunted. "I guess the guy must've used a handkerchief when he made the stab. Maybe he didn't have gloves. So his little finger got outside the handkerchief and left the print."

"So what?" I choraled.

"My God!" Hanley groaned. "We get a print and he asks, 'So what?' Listen, pencil-pusher, I'm taking this print down to h.q. and down there I'm going to check it. When I have learned who it belongs to I will make an arrest and this time your face will be redder than an albino's sunburn. Are you gonna come along?"

"My, my," I said, "what a policeman you've become since I made you a lieutenant! No, I'm not coming along. You take it and when you had to find that print among your collection of doo-dabs, I may be able to let you in on a few things."

"Yah!" Poppa grinned. "Whistling in the dark this time, Daffy."

As a matter of fact, I was. But I didn't want to let him know it. Professional pride or something. And just then, as luck would have it, my orbs fell on the green blotter which covered Benny Cassell's desk, and when I saw what I saw I grinned at him from ear to ear, the ole fight returning to the little gray cells. Benny had scribbled a name on the blotter. It wasn't the name of the killer, because Benny hadn't even thought he would be killed. It was the name of an undertaker.

I chortled, "Whistling in the dark. Poppa? Why how can you say that? You know I don't go out nights, and I can't whistle a taxi. Take your little print down to h.q. and I'll call you there in time to make the arrest."

I started for the door.

"Hey!" Hanley called, frowning. "Where you going?"

"Sleuthing," I said sarcastically.

"Where?"

"A newspaperman is not compelled to divulge—"

"Okay, okay," Hanley said balefully. "Go on and prowl. But for the sake of the Bureau of Vital Statistics, tell the guy who gives you the slug to let us know where we can find your young corpse."

"My pal," I said, drawing my index finger over my throat. I slammed the door of the office, waved a chipper bon voyage to the Fisher gel, and was on my way.

I ducked into the first public phone booth I saw and grabbed a directory. The name Benny Cassell had written was Sharpe Brothers. I found their number in the book and dropped a nickel in the slot and called them. Needless to say, Sharpe Brothers is an establishment for the fixing-upping of fashionable bodies, and is located on East Fifty-Ninth Street.

A metallic voice said, "Sharpe's!"

"Give me the cashier's department," I said gruffly.

There were a couple of nice, earbreaking slams on the other end of the wire. Then a gal's voice said: "Ye-as?"

"Cashier's department?" I asked.

"The same."

"This is the Coroner's office, City of New York," I said importantly. "We're investigating the death of one Dollie Merritt, and we'd like some information from you."

"Oh, yes," said the gal breathlessly. "What is it?"

"We'd like to know who paid the funeral and cremation expenses of Miss Merritt."

"Just a moment." There was a short pause while she looked it up for me. When she came back, she said:

"Hello? According to our records the expense was handled by her attending physician, Dr. Ralph Planey of Stanley Place."

I said genially, "My friend, that's all I wanted to know," and I hung up with a bang. Out in the street, I hailed a hack and clambered in. "Stanley Place, speed king, and no fooling around," I told the driver.

Only then, as we roared away in a cloud of dust, did I realize that some one was tailing me. I caught just a glimpse of the bird, a long angular guy with a broken nose, as he bounced into another cab and roared after me. I watched him through the back window cautiously, but I couldn't make out his pan. All I could catch was the broken schnozzle. He tailed me and no error. I had my driver circle the block twice and the other hack did just the same.

I shrugged it off and headed for the main rendezvous. It took us nearly half an hour to reach Stanley Place. Traffic was thick. When we got there, I found that the spot where Dr. Planey spent his nights was an apartment house, and a snoozy one at that.

Paying off the hack driver, I went in and to the elevator bank. The tailer with the broken nose had disappeared. I figured he was hiding somewhere outside the place, waiting for me to show up again. I took the elevator up to the ninth floor and got out. Then I rang Dr. Planey's bell and waited.

4

TWO CAN BE SMART

I DIDN'T PARK the tootsies long. He opened right up. He was a guy of medium height, a trifle gray at the temples, and immaculately dressed. The skin of his face seemed to shine. He wore a pince-nez with a black ribbon on it which hung back over his right ear. And he had fish-eyes. Big black irises without any expression. I didn't like them at all.

"Yes?" he asked.

I flashed the tin detectatif badge which I picked up in a hockshop on Fourteenth Street for a dime once, and which same has more than once been a good bluff and an exit out of a jam.

"Holmes is my handle," I said.

"Homicide bureau. I'm investigating the death of Dollie Merritt. We had a tip there might have been foul play and the chief thought I'd better take a run up and see you and get the real info."

His jaw twitched slightly as his fisheyes gave me a thorough once-over. "Foul play?" he said crisply. "Nonsense! Won't you step in?"

I stepped. He had a nice layout, but what caught my eye right off was the nice walnut desk across the living room. That was my meat. I took a chair close to it.

He rubbed his hands. "Now—"

"I'll talk," I said brusquely, imitating old walrus-faced Inspector Halloran as best I could. "When did you go onto that case?"

"A week ago," Dr. Planey replied. "I was Miss Merritt's medico for the past two years. On last Sunday morning she felt severe pain and called me. When I got there I learned that she had eaten some lobster which she had left in the can for three days. She had a bad case of ptomaine. I attended her, but nothing much could be done. She grew weaker and three days ago went into pneumonia. She died yesterday."

"And was cremated today," I said.

"Yes," he nodded, looking surprised. "That's correct."

"And you handled the cost of the thing," I said. "Why?"

He shifted uncomfortably and avoided my eyes. "I always liked the girl. She was very sweet. She died penniless. She had no people. I couldn't stand the thought of a burial for her in Potter's Field, so I shouldered the expense. Just a whim of mine."

"Think of that," I said dryly. "And was it just a whim of yours to have her body burned immediately so there could be no exhumation nor autopsy?"

"Really!" he snapped.

"And," I added, "you know damn well she was nothing but a chiseller and a blackmailer. Sweet girl my eye! She'd have taken the shirt off your back if she had had the chance. Listen, doc, there's no green in my glimmers, see? Now who was it died yesterday?"

"Dollie Merritt," he said, puzzled.

"Sure, sure," I waved. "But, on the level, between you

and me who was it died? Who was the kid they burned in Dollie Merritt's place? Who was the kid who looked like Dollie Merritt and was made the fall-guy? Why was that done? What's the racket?"

"You're insulting!" Dr. Planey growled. "I don't have to take this from anyone!" He nervously lighted a cigarette. "And the theory is asinine. Medicos don't do that sort of thing."

"Right the first time," I said. "But a medico who'd work as sawbones for a mob of hoods might do anything, savvy, doc?"

He paled a trifle and jammed his cigarette in an ash tray. "How did you find that out?"

"I get around," I said. "East side, West side."

He stared at me a long time without speaking. His fish-eyes were still void of any expression. Finally a thin smile slit his lips. "Excuse me for a few minutes, won't you?" he said, and turned abruptly and left the room.

I wasted no time. I'd prayed for a break like this and hadn't expected to get it. I wanted to look through that desk. I didn't know quite what I'd find, but I had them thar hunches that it would be very interesting.

In the top drawer I found a brown manila envelope. It was a bank statement for the doc from his checking account. I yanked it out and glanced at it. It was opened. I pulled the canceled checks and the statement out. I thumbed through the checks and a name hit me right in the eye. Footsteps sounded in the next room. I jerked the top drawer shut and stuffed the statement and checks and envelope in my pockets. Dr. Planey came back in just as I reached my chair again.

He looked pleased with himself. "Is there anything else," he asked smilingly, "which you would like to ask?"

I shrugged. "You'll only lie. What's the use? I'll shove off, doc. But you haven't heard the last of this."

He smiled again and opened the door. "Nor have you, Mr. Daffy Dill. Nor have you. Remember, people are not always as dumb as you think they are."

"Nice going," I said. "But you didn't recognize me. It took the guy you telephoned to tell you I was here." That was just a blind stab, but he flushed when I said it and I knew I'd hit a bull's-eye. I nodded to him and went out the door."

He said, "So long, Dill."

"See you in jail," I said.

I TOOK ANOTHER hack the instant I hit the street and I waved a ripe fin under the driver's nose and asked for speed to shake off the guy with the broken nose who hopped right on my tail. We lost him after a four-block zigzag, and then I looked over the doc's checks.

Most of these checks were bills and such. But two of them hit me in the eye like the spoon in my coffee. They were made out to *Ronald Fortney!* Which same, if you will kindly recall, was the ex-hubby of the supposedly-deceased Dollie Merritt. One of the checks was for a two-century figure. The other was for half a grand. The half a grand one had been cashed by Fortney and endorsed by him in Hollywood, California. The other one—for two hundred bucks—had been endorsed by him payable to the American Home Assurance Company of 85 Broadway in payment on policy No. 445690.

Right there was the works as plain as Miami Beach in

the sun. I put the checks away and headed for my own apartment on West Forty-Sixth Street. It didn't take long. Maybe twenty minutes. I paid off the driver, took one last look around to make sure I had lost the guy with the broken nose, and then I went in and up the four flights to the spot I call home.

I hit the handset right away and called the American Home Assurance Company. It was close to five o'clock and I worked fast to get them before closing. They crashed through. I said:

"Death claim department, please."

In a few seconds: "Hello? Death claims."

"This is Holmes, Homicide bureau," I said gruffly. "Investigating death of one Dollie Merritt. I understand she had a policy with you. Check on it, please, and let me have the data."

"Just a moment, please." It was a male clerk, and he kept me waiting more than a moment. A full five minutes went by before he came back. He asked, "What do you wish to know, Mr. Holmes?"

"What was she insured for?"

"One hundred thousand dollars."

I whistled. "Now ain't that something! And who paid the premiums!"

"Ronald Fortney."

"Who was beneficiary?"

"The same. He's her ex-husband."

"You're telling *me?*" I took a breath. "Hokey, friend. When will the death claim be paid and where?"

"It has been paid," said the clerk. "This morning we handed the check to Mr. Fortney. It is a policy of our company that death-claim money is in the hands of the beneficiary within twenty-four hours, and we—"

"Never mind the sales talk," I snapped. "Where did you pay the mazuma? Where is Fortney parking the carcass?"

"At the Pickwick Arms on West Fiftieth Street."

"Good," I said, "and where—"

I never finished the question. I heard one thing—the squeak of my apartment door opening. I never lock the damn thing. I started to wheel around for a glam at the would-be intruder when something like the bottom of an army tank hit me across the top of the head, wrenching my fedora from my Greek skull and slamming me neatly off the chair to the floor, flat on my back. That was the works. I never saw anything. I never even heard anything. All I remember doing was falling and dropping the telephone in the flight....

When I came to, I had the kind of headache a rhinoceros gets when a hunter puts a slug into the base of the lethal horn. I sat up, groaning, and felt my head. I felt swollen like four hangovers.

"Ah me," I said. "This night life—" I looked around. A young interne in white pants and coat was grinning at me, and a blue-coated flat-foot was standing across the room. I said, "Hello, palsies. Explain please."

"You were shot," the interne said, and still grinned.

"Ha ha ha," I said solemnly. "And what's so funny about that?"

"The fact that you're alive," said the interne. "You oughta be dead, and that's no kidding. The bullet parted your hair like a barber. An inch lower and—phoof!"

"Yeah," I said. "Just like that." I glanced around. "Damn funny. I didn't hear any shot."

"You wouldn't when the slug hit you like that. Just like a blackjack. You were out before the sound started. Who did it?"

"I dunno," I said. "I didn't see a soul. How did you birds get up here, anyhow?"

"The operator heard the shot," the cop said. "She had the number traced and called for police and an ambulance. She was a smart kid, if you ask me."

"If you ask me," I said, "I agree with you. She's an unsung hero and I don't feel so chipper. And now, if you will pardon me, gents, there is work to be done. I am alive, if not well. I do not know the reason for this felonious assault and I did not see my attacker. Thanks one and all for your trouble." I paused. "Catch on?"

"He wants us to scram," said the interne to the cop.

"I'm for it," the cop said. They gathered themselves together and departed down the four flights.

5

THE SILVER SLIPPER

I STILL FELT wozzy, but kind of sore, too. I hadn't expected the other side to start playing for keeps so soon and so dexterously. It left me a little breathless. I sat down, facing the door this time, and I called the *Chronicle* office. I got Dinah Mason right off the bat.

I said, "Listen, Angel-Eyes. I'm on a beat. It's tough going, so tough that I've already dodged a slug which has left a part across my young cranium. So it's serious, understand?"

"Daffy!" Dinah cried, alarmed. "Are you all right?"

"Then you will marry me?" I said.

"No. Are you kidding? Daffy, if you've—"

"No, kid," I said. "On the level. I've been shot, but I'm hokey now. Here's what I want you to do. Tell the morgue to get out every news-story they have on Dollie Merritt. And, above all, get a picture of the blonde chiseller. A picture, photo, get it? I need it like Romeo needed Juliet. If they haven't got one in the morgue, tell 'em to get one. I'm on my way down. Got it?"

"Right!" she clipped.

"Then get to work," I said, and hung up. I lifted the

handset immediately and called police headquarters, asking for the homicide bureau and Poppa Hanley.

I said, "Poppa, war has been declared!"

"Listen," he replied, "did you get anything, Daffy?"

He sounded too eager. "What's the matter?" I asked. "Didn't your print turn out?"

"Naw," he said reluctantly. "Guess you were right. We didn't have it on file at all. What's this stuff about war?"

"I've been shot," I said. "Now don't fly off the handle. I'm all right. But the fact remains that after I made a visit to the home of Dr. Ralph Planey some guy gunned me at me own spot. So do me a favor. Put a shadow on Doc Ralph Planey and keep a shadow on him. We want reports on every spot Planey visits from now on. He's in this thing hand and foot, Poppa. Planey is the guy who handled the Merritt cremation expense. Planey is the guy who paid the premiums on her life insurance through Ronald Fortney, her ex, who is also in this. Planey is the guy who gave Fortney the money to come east from Hollywood. Get that?"

Hanley just gasped.

"Yeah," I said. "Fortney is in our fair city. Apparently he anticipated the fact that Dollie Merritt was going to die. He arrived here just in time to get a sweet one hundred grand insurance check handed over to him. Do you get the whole lay now?"

"I'll say I do!" Hanley warbled hoarsely. "It's a swindle and there's murder in it. Dollie Merritt, her ex, and this sawbones, Planey, figured a nice way to make a hundred thou'. They find a gal along the night spots who looks just like Dollie—"

"Except," I interrupted, "the gal has *red hair instead of blonde.*"

"Right," said Hanley. "Don't stop me. I'm hot. They see this gal and they're all broke. One of 'em gets an idea how to make coin. The ex-husband is called in on it, and, being as crooked as the medico and the chorine, he signs. He takes out the policy on Dollie's life, with Planey financing the thing with his last capital. Then they snatch this other gal—the one who looks like Dollie—and they dye her hair blonde. They feed her some food that gives her ptomaine and they slowly let her die until it turns into pneumonia. Meanwhile the real Dollie gets a henna and takes the name and place of the dying gal. So 'Dollie' dies and the coin goes to Fortney, who holds it for a three-way split. And when that coin is split, Daffy, the three cons will lam!"

"Poppa," I marveled, "you have covered the ground adequately. You get smarter and smarter and some day I will have you made an inspector. You've spilled it. That's the way it happened."

"But I haven't got a damn piece of evidence to hoosegow the eggs," Hanley moaned. "That's where I'm stumped. One of them bumped Benny Cassell. They had to do that. He saw Dollie on the street and recognized her. He was the only catch in the plan."

"You'll have your evidence before dawn," I said. "Just follow the instructions I gave you. Tail Planey. Don't let him out of sight."

"By God!" Hanley exclaimed sharply. "I'll handle it myself. And what are you gonna do?"

"Me?" I said. "I'm on the Dawn Patrol tonight, Poppa. This Dollie was a chorine. The gal who they substituted for her and who is now ashes to ashes, might've been a chorine, too. Birds of a feather and all that hooey. Right now, I'm going down to the *Chronicle*, get a photo of La Merritt's chiseling pan, and study it until I'm pink and blue in the face. And after I've studied it, it'll be the Dawn Patrol for me. I'll cover every giggle-water front on the great divide and I won't come back until I find that dame, henna or no henna!"

IT WAS ONE A.M., when the night owls frolic, and still no sign of Dollie Merritt. Alone and unaided and making a pretense of taking little gossip notes about the luminaries of Broadway for Harry Lyons' alleged colyum, I had visited every honky-tonk from Fifty-Ninth Street down to Forty-Fourth.

And I was getting tired of dancing nudes, giggle-water, bright and soft lights, and sweet music....

I turned in at Bill Latham's Hideaway Club for an Old-Fashioned to pep me up. And no sooner had Bill caught sight of me than he waved me into his private office—the modernistic job which is oh so swell—with my drink and all. When I got in and squatted in the most comfortable chair, he handed me his telephone and said, "Call Hanley."

"Huh?" I said.

"Call Hanley," said Latham again. "He buzzed me around midnight. Said for you to get in touch with him the moment you came in."

"My, my," I said, "where is he now?"

Latham shrugged. "I don't make it out. Said he'd be at the home of Dr. Planey until you called. He figured you might wander in here sometime tonight. What's the case, Daffy?"

"That Dollie Merritt business," I said. "You were all wrong on it, Bill. I guess you know we found Benny Cassell murdered about an hour or two after he was in here this afternoon?"

Latham paled. "No!"

"Sure," I said. "He saw a ghost walking and the ghost didn't like it. And you thought he was hopped. It just goes to show that the Dill hunch has never been denied. Look up Planey's number in the phone book for me, will you? The address is Stanley Place."

Dumfounded, Latham looked it up and gave it to me. I put through a call for Hanley and got him right off. "Poppa," I said, "this is the prodigal son. What you want, hah?"

"Listen, Daffy," Hanley replied earnestly, "this is no time for wisecracks. Planey is dead."

I sat bolt-upright and nearly drank the glass and all when I finished my Old-Fashioned.

"*What?*"

"Oh, for God's sake," Hanley said, annoyed. "Don't act surprised. Planey is dead. He's been bumped off. A .32 did the job. I came over here to tail him when he left his joint. I stood around half the night and he never came out. I was getting tired of waiting when a bellboy came tooting out, yelling for cops. When I got upstairs there he was. Point-blank shot right through the head, with powder burns. No sign of the rod. No sign of anything. The killer who pulled this one is way in the clear. Nobody saw anybody or even heard anything." He sighed. "How're things with you?"

"Stalemate," I said. "I haven't found a thing. Listen, Poppa, Planey has received the well-known doublecross. He was bumped off so's that insurance check would be split two ways instead of three!"

"You don't say," Hanley replied sarcastically. "My, but that's brilliant deduction, coming from you!"

I said, "You're sore, Poppa. Don't blame you. But don't take it out on me. It isn't my fault that criminals clutter up this burg. I'll be right over. Stand by."

I hung up and waved to Latham. "See you, Bill. Thanks."

"Killing?" he asked.

"This is the third in this case," I said. "Isn't it funny what some people will do for fifty grand apiece?" I left his office and when I hit the sidewalk on Broadway in front of the Hideaway who should I get a glimpse of but my shadow— the guy with the broken nose.

Unconsciously I stiffened, remembering the slug which had parted my hair that afternoon. I stood there a second; then changed my mind about the hack I was going to take. I figured the time had come for a showdown and I was itching to wrap my paws around my shadow's throat. You know—the skin you love to clutch.

Turning right, I walked toward Forty-Third Street, watching the show windows along the way to see whether Broken Nose would follow through. He did. He picked up his heels and laid them down again right on my trail. When I reached the corner of Forty-Third, I turned east toward Fifth Avenue—but I didn't keep on walking. Instead, I ducked the second I got around the corner and I waited there.

Broken Nose was a sucker. He came around the corner

like a snow plough, wide open, and afraid he might lose track of me. He nearly bumped into me. When he saw me he stopped dead, and his big jaw dropped until I thought it would smack the pavement.

I stuck my right hand in my coat pocket, made a rod-barrel out of my index finger, and jammed him in the ribs with it. I snapped, "Easy does it, Rasputin, easy does it!"

HE RELAXED, STARING at me. His nose was sure broken, a big flat thing with an indent in the middle. He said hoarsely, "What'cha gonna do?"

"Why the tail?" I asked sharply.

He wet his lips. "I kinda thought—maybe—"

"Spill, spill," I snapped, "or I'll have you in the can for the shot you fired at me this aft'."

"Shot I fired at—" He stopped. "Hey, mister, don't get me wrong. I didn't fire no shot at yuh!"

"At my flat this aft'," I reminded. "When I left Doc Planey's."

"Brother, you're screwy!" he said. "I lost yuh after yuh left Planey's. Yuh shook me off."

That was the truth.

"What's more," he added, "I don't know where yuh hang out. I don't even know yuh moniker!"

"Then why tail me?" I snapped.

"Well," he said, "I kinda thought maybe you knew something about this Merritt case."

"Suppose I do. What's it to you?"

He didn't answer. I nudged him with my finger. "Come across, Adonis, and make it snappy. I want info. Who are you?"

"The moniker is Hogan," he said, growling.

"And the racket?"

He flashed a badge, and it was genuine! "Special investigator for American Home Life Assurance Company," he said.

"And you're on the Merritt case?"

"Yeah."

"Then why follow me around?"

"I—kinda thought—maybe you knew somethin' about it."

I laughed. "Listen, you cluck, I am Daffy Dill, far-famed member of the Fourth Estate, and no insurance swindler as you've been kidding yourself into thinking."

He groaned. "Daffy Dill? Oh, jeeze, and I been shadowin'—"

"Never mind the hearts and flowers," I said. "I still want info. Haven't you tailed this Ronald Fortney at all?"

Hogan nodded. "I tailed 'em all. Fortney. Planey. Cassell. You. I figured one of yuh might know somethin' and whadda I get? Dead alleys."

"You tailed Fortney?" I asked. "Swanky. Where does he hang out?"

"Pickwick Arms Hotel. How about takin' that rod away?"

"That's no rod," I said. "I was only bluffing. And I didn't mean where he stayed. Where does he hang out?"

"Night life, yuh mean?"

I nodded.

"He only goes to one spot to enjoy himself. The Silver Slipper on West Forty-Second."

"Hot canine!" I yodelled. "Mister, am I glad to meet you! Come along with me and your insurance company will be in a hundred grand before the night is over."

I dragged him after me and we went down Broadway like a pair of maniacs. On the way I stopped in at one of those clip-joint jewelers and bought a cheap black enameled cigarette case, which I carefully wiped with a hankie and put away.

When we reached the Silver Slipper, I parked Hogan outside and told him to wait. I went in. A guy named Micky Harris ran the joint. I didn't know him at all, since it was a super-smart spot which cost money. Thus, I never frequented it.

It was a smooth place. The dance floor looked like the armory of the Seventh Regiment, and they had a bar against one wall that stretched nearly a city block. I hit the bar right away and drank an Old-Fashioned while I awaited developments. A pair of Latins from Manhattan were can-canning all over the place under a blue spotlight.

Somebody bumped my arm and I got a whiff of alkie which nearly gave me a second-hand jag. I glanced at the bird and found it to be Toby Claghorn, a young man about town who has plenty of rocks and wants to have plenty of ladies. He was badly in his cups and he looked as though he were going to cry.

I said cheerfully, "Hello, playboy, remember me?"

Toby stared at me a moment and said sorrowfully, "Daffy Dill in th' flesh."

"Right the first time," I said. "Why so dismal?"

He hiccupped. "She doesn't love me anymore."

"Who doesn't love you?"

"Margie Kenny."

"Who's she?" I asked.

"The bes' dancer in New Yawk! The bes' lil dancer and the swedes' lil red-head—"

I went stiff. "Red-head, Toby?" I repeated.

"Pos'tively Titian!" he slurred thickly. "Jus' a lovely lil girl. She doesn' love me anymore. Las' week she was crazy 'bout me. This week, she doesn' love me anymore...."

I turned to the bartender. "Hey, Mac, who's Margie Kenny?"

"Solo rhumba," said the bartender. "She comes on soon. She ain't bad, mister, not bad at all. She shakes a mean hoof."

"Toby," I said, "this Margie, your red-head, have you noticed anything changed about her face or the tone of her voice in the last week?"

"I was tellin' you," he said with difficulty. "She doesn' pay any 'tention to me anymore. Ever since las' week. My heart is broken. All she does is dance with that Fortney fella and—"

"Hold it," I said swiftly. To the bartender again:

"Mac, did this Kenny dame miss a night last week?"

"Yeah," he said. "Wednesday."

"That's got it," I said. "Thanks."

The house lights dimmed as a voice in the semi-darkness announced:

"—presenting now Miss Margie Kenny in her own version of Cuba's fiery rhumba—" A baby spot leaped into being, making a patch of silver on the dance floor. I walked away from reeling Toby Claghorn, and watched for the gel's entrance.

6

THE CHORINE

THE MUSIC FLARED. From a doorway across the floor she flashed onto the floor in a stunning black satin gown replete with dazzling sequins which threw back the spotlight in millions of blazing diamonds. She went into her dance. There was Margie Kenny, the henna-haired chorine of the Slipper Show. At least, that's what the customers thought and believed.

But I saw someone else, and I felt tingles seethe down my spine as chills studded my flesh with pimples.

I'd spent three hours on the photo of Dollie Merritt which the *Chronicle* morgue had dug up for me. Three hours surveying one female pan and I'd have known it anywhere. The real Margie Kenny was deader than Napoleon's grandpa. She was dust, cremated that a.m. at the Ferncliff furnaces. And out on the floor, a corpse was dancing to the infectious rhythms of *La Cucaracha*. Dead Dollie Merritt was out there, shaking her legs in a rhumba.

I smiled thinly.

Dollie Merritt was dead in name only. A corpse, she was worth a hundred grand to Ronald Fortney and herself. Alive, they were penniless. It had been a hot play, and it had worked. Margie Kenny, Benny Cassell, Doc Planey, they were all dead. Margie died because she looked too much like La Merritt. Benny died because he recognized a walking body. Planey died because of a double-cross. And Dollie and Fortney were in the money.

I edged around the floor until I reached the door through which Dollie had made her entrance. I stood here and watched her go through the rest of her act. It was good. It got a big hand. I clapped myself and when she gave them a little encore, I took out the cigarette case which I had bought on the way over and I gave it another wipe-off.

She finished her encore and the lights came up as she wheeled and made for the door where I lolled.

"Excuse me, Miss Kenny?" I said.

She looked at me and smiled. Boy, she was hard! She'd done her best to fix her pan so's she'd look like the sweet young thing Margie Kenny had probably been, but there were bags under her eyes and a jut to her jaw that was plain nasty. And her eyes—violet things with funny kinds of gleams in them—were too furtive to be on the level. When she smiled, I shivered. She asked, "Yeah?"

I held out the black enamel case. "I found this right here after you'd come in. Thought maybe you'd dropped it. You didn't, did you?"

She took it automatically and turned it over, looking at it. She said nicely, "Why no, it isn't mine. Thank you. It was very considerate of you to think I'd dropped it."

I wrapped my hankie around the case and put it away. "Think nothing of it, Dollie," I said. "I'm a very considerate guy."

She stiffened like a ramrod and blanched a little under her grease paint. "What did you say?"

"I said—think nothing of it, Dollie."

"My name's Margie Kenny," she snapped.

"Ah, no!" I said innocently, wagging my finger. "That's all right for the paying customers. But not for Daffy Dill."

"Daffy Dill!" she rapped, grabbing at her throat and staring at me.

"Alive and well, thank you," I said. "So sorry, Dollie, but the ex held his rod too high. He did a better job on Doc Planey, though. That makes fifty grand for you and fifty grand for Ronnie, doesn't it? Bad, though. Too, too bad that you'll never spend it."

"What is this?" she asked evenly, her jaw sticking out like the bowsprit of a schooner. "A gag?"

"No gag, Dollie. On the level. You and the ex are through. This very night thou and he will repose within the damp confines of one of our better jugs."

She was trembling now, but had the nerve to hold the stance. "I told you my name was Margie Kenny. And I don't know what you're raving about."

"You can say you're Margie from now until Roosevelt is elected again for all I care. But fingerprints don't lie, Dollie. Catchee on? You just put your prints all over the cigarette case I handed you. Said cigarette case is about to go down to Centre Street, where said prints will be checked with those of one Dollie Merritt, chiseller and blackmailer supreme. And the swell part is—they'll match!"

I tweaked her cheek pleasantly. "So long, swindler. And remember, when murder has been committed, an accessory before or after the fact roasts just as nicely as a Rhode Island red."

I LEFT HER there and went right over to the bar where I

slipped the bartender a fin and said quickly, "Mac, fire-works are about to let go. For that fin, do me two favors."

"Who do you want me to kill?"

"Nix," I said. "There's a mug outside who answers to the name of Hogan. Tell him Daffy Dill is in trouble and tell him to come right to Margie Kenny's dressing room with his rod out. Got that?"

"I—got it," the bartender swallowed. "Are you on the level?"

"After that," I said, ignoring his query, "telephone Lieutenant Bill Hanley of the homicide squad and tell him that Daffy Dill is in trouble at the Silver Slipper. When he gets here, send him into the same dressing room. And make it snappy."

Without looking around, I left the bar and started for the nearest exit. I knew I wouldn't reach it. I hadn't taken four steps before the muzzle of a .32 poked me meaningly in the side and a smooth voice said:

"Stop dead and act friendly."

I turned. He was a handsome ginzo, tall, lean-faced, with black hair as shiny as oil. His skin had a healthy tan from a California sun. I had to smile. Dollie Merritt had wasted no time in getting the bad news over to this bird. He must've been waiting in her room when she went back after her routine. I smiled. "If it isn't Ronnie Fortney! All dressed up fit to kill."

"You guessed that last right," he said, his white teeth grating. "No tricks, Dill, or I'll cook you right here. You know I mean it, too."

"Sure," I said. "See the part in my hair? That ought to show that you mean it." I chuckled. "It was only ten feet.

You must be a lousy shot. You had to get Planey at point-blank range to hit him."

The .32 kicked into my ribs. "It's at pointblank range right now," Fortney said evenly. "Suppose we go back to Margie's dressing room."

"You mean Dollie's," I said.

He shrugged, "Have it your own way. Go ahead."

I went. It was a short trip through the curtained door down a corridor. He opened her dressing room door without knocking. He hit the muzzle of the gun in me again and I moved inside. He came right after me, closing the door. Dollie Merritt, who had been pacing nervously back and forth, stopped and glared at me.

"You got him?" she said venomously.

"I got him," Fortney said.

"Did you get the cigarette case?" she asked.

The gun nudged me. "Hand it over, sucker." I dug it out and handed it over. Dollie took it and wiped it clean.

"Well, Ron," she said, "what now?"

Out on the dance floor, the band had struck into the rampant Continental. The sound of the brasses came back to us distinctly. Ronald Fortney looked grim. "You have the bag?"

"Right here," she said, patting a black valise. "No one's been near it since you went after this mug."

"We're blowing," Fortney said. "This town is too hot. If you didn't have a record at h.q., we might bluff the thing out. As it is, your prints will give the play away sure. No reason why we shouldn't take a powder. The cash is there safe and sound. Get some clothes together. We'll take a train west. Then maybe around the world until the heat is turned off."

She threw a wad of scanties into a small bag. The operation didn't take three minutes. When she was finished, she put the bag next to the valise on the floor. "Oke," she said. She nodded to him. "What about your stuff at the hotel?"

"I'm leaving it," Fortney said. "No telling how far this mug has gone with his hunches."

She shrugged. "And what about him?"

"He gets it right here and now before he can sing to anybody else," Fortney said coldly.

"Oh, please spare me!" I chirped. "Remember my gray-haired mother and my frau and my fourteen children!"

"Can it," Dollie snapped. "But, Ron—the shot—"

Fortney smiled. "Hear that music? It'll make a swell soundscreen. Nobody'll hear a thing. Do you know where the back door is?" She nodded. "Good. You take your own bag. I'll carry the cash." He pushed me forward. "Take it sitting down, Dill. That chair right there.

I don't want a thud when you hit."

I sat down in a chair next to the dressing table, facing the gun and the door.

"I don't want to see this," Dollie said suddenly.

"Then get outside," snapped Fortney. "Wait for me right outside. Be ready to blow when you hear the shot. Now scram."

DOLLIE NODDED, RUBBING her hand across her mouth. She picked up both of the bags and slowly walked across the room toward the door. At the door, she put the money-bag down and turned the knob. She glanced back at me, a sneer curling her lips. She said, "I'll say this for you, sucker.

You figured it all the way and it's tough you can't write it.
It'd make a hot scoop. Give my best to Margie Kenny."

"I'll do that, chiseller," I said, watching sharply.

She chuckled and opened the door.

Instantly she let go a bloodcurdling shriek which sent
the hairs on my neck sticking out like a porcupine's back! It
was sheer fright, that shriek, and its sincerity was its horror!

Ronald Fortney, who had been facing me, holding the
gun in a bead on my young chest, whirled around toward
her like a top, the suddenness of Dollie's terror scaring him
half to death.

That was all I needed.

I dove headlong at his knees, right out of the chair, and
I hit him like a right tackle. You could hear the resonance
of the thud as we both slammed against the floor, rolling
like logs.

The force of the tackle knocked the .32 out of Fortney's
hand and it flew through the air with the greatest of ease
right over by the dressing table.

I clawed at Fortney as he climbed to his feet and we
began to jab each other. He didn't know much about it. He
kept swinging long shots at me which went over the top
of my bean. To an outsider, however, it might have looked
as though he were killing me.

That's the way it was. Hogan, who had been waiting
outside the door with a big .45 Colt in his paw, figured
that I was getting the works from Fortney. He squeezed the
trigger of the rod. A resounding crash hit each of the four
walls. Bitter smoke billowed in right under my nose. In
front of me, Ronald Fortney contorted, his chest shooting
forward as the slug caught him in the back and dropped

him to the floor on his face. He never made a sound. But on the floor, he writhed like a snake. A bullet which breaks the spine is a damned ugly thing.

But Hogan forgot Dollie Merritt. As soon as she had recovered from the momentary fright she had when she came face to face with him, she fell back into the room and watched Fortney and I square off. When the .32 was flung over by the dressing table, she went after it.

The next thing I knew after Fortney started twisting on the floor, my hat made a one-way trip against the opposite wall. Dollie was firing the little .32 as fast as she could work the trigger. Another slug buzzed by my ear and I nearly caught cold from the breeze.

Hogan yelped. He got one shot at her before she nipped him. I saw his gun drop to the floor as he went to his knees, his face contorted in pain.

It was a spot. She was as blind as a bat and as crazy as a loon. There was only one way to stop her and I took it. I took it fast.

Hogan's rod was out of reach and out of the question.

The only thing I saw was a bottle of liquid hair-set, greenish stuff which Dollie had used to make waves in her hair. It was standing on the dressing table. There was a chair between the table and me. I did a neat jacknife so that I landed behind yon chair.

My dive caught the blonde redhead's attention and her rod barked a couple of times, making the nicest little holes in the wall just over my back. Snaking my right hand onto the table from behind the chair, I grabbed the bottle of hair-set and winged it at her snarling pan with all I had.

It cracked her squarely on the chin. She went out cold, flat on her back, still gripping the smoking gun.

Hogan was groaning. I got up and tore over to him.

"Where did she get you?" I snapped.

"Lookit, by damn!" he wailed. "My gun hand! She had to go put a slug through my gun hand. And me such a lousy southpaw with a roscoe!"

I could have kissed his busted schnozzle. The only thing wrong with him was a clean wound right through the palm of his right paw. Otherwise he was safe and serene.

I don't know what happened to Hanley. When he finally arrived, Fortney was already in *rigor mortis* and Dollie was still on ice, out cold.

It developed later on that Fortney was the guy who had slipped the blade into Benny Cassell, taken the nick at me, and put the slug on Planey. He had cashed the insurance check, too. The coin was all in the black bag.

Which all goes to show—as I wrote in Harry Lyons' colyum the next day—corpses can sometimes dance after they have been cremated. And when you are scanning obituaries on a bright and cheerful day, you can't always believe what you read in the newspapers.

MAN BITES DOG

"I Want Someone to Murder Me," Said the Broker—and to Daffy Dill That Was the First Step in an Extraordinary Crime

1

THE BUMPER-OFFER SUPREME

THE OLD MAN was mad. He wasn't boiling. He was just normally and fiendishly sarcastic. His lumbago was probably bothering him, so he called me into his doghouse to tell me what a rotten scribe I'd turned out to be. That always made the lumbago feel better.

"Sometimes," he said nastily, "even the best of us start to slip, Daffy."

I said, "Speak for yourself, John."

"I'm speaking," he returned with fire, "about the way you earn your forty-five shekels per week on this newspaper. Only you don't earn them."

I looked hurt. "Why, Rasputin, how can you say that? And me so sensitive about my earning power?"

"Ha-ha," he mourned, grating his teeth. "It occurred to me that perhaps I'd better instruct you again in the precepts of good reporting. It has been slightly over a week since I read anything from your lopsided typewriter which had even a slight aroma of news. Do you catch on?"

"When you speak English, I do," I said. "And what the hell do you expect me to do—scoop the world every week?"

I was beginning to catch on. Not only was it his lumbago, it was also the fact that the past week had been one of those all-quiet-on-the-New-York-front ones. I'd scoured the fair city and I hadn't turned up anything big at all. That's the joy of being too good. Guys get to expect a batting average of a hundred per cent.

"I don't expect you," said the Old Man, "to scoop the world—ever." The sarcasm was in good form. It dripped venom. "All I'm asking you is that you remember certain definite things. I am under the sad impression that you are beginning to fail to recognize news when it slaps you in the face. Now if a dog—"

"Holy, holy, holy!" I murmured. "If you give me that again this year they'll put me in a nut jug. When a man bites a dog, that's news. When a dog bites a man, that's hydrophobia."

"So you've heard that before?" The Old Man sneered.

"You know what?" I said. "Ever since they taught me that when I was a cub I've always looked for the guy who would be nutty enough to bite a dog. And I've never found him." I grinned at him. "How about you, Chief? We could stage a show in Central Park and maybe I'd get a raise?"

BEFORE HE HAD a chance to tell me that I'd been sitting on my brains so long they were getting flat, the telephone on his desk jingled. He eyed me balefully and picked up the handset, still trying to figure out a snappy comeback. "Desk speaking," he said. "Eh? Yeah, he's here, I'm sorry to say." He glanced at me. "It's Dinah, out front. She says there's a call for you."

I shrugged. "I'm not proud. I'll use your phone, despite the rabies bacilli on the mouthpiece. Hand over, plizz."

The Old Man sighed in defeat and threw the handset at me, expertly aiming it at my tender schnozzola. I averted

*The window was
unlocked and half open*

catastrophe by stabbing it out of thin air and placing it delicately against my left ear.

"Hello?" I said.

Dinah's voice came through. "Hello, Dracula. Here's your party."

"So sweet of you," I replied jeeringly and then I listened while she clicked the call in. It was a man. His voice was sort of hoarse and soft, and he sounded pretty jittery.

"I want Dill," he said. "Daffy Dill. I won't talk with anyone but him."

"My fran," I said. "Daffy Dill is hearkening to your words at this very minute."

"Is this you, Dill?"

"No kidding, it is."

"This is Londo." The voice got huskier. "Nicky Londo."

"Yeah?" I said. I tipped my hat way back on my head and frowned. Nicky Londo had once been known as the Killer of Broadway. That was in the days of good beer, you know, pre repeal. I didn't know the monkey personally. Nicky Londo had dropped out of the headlines and out of the racket when drinking became legal. But from what I had picked up, Nicky Londo was a tough baby.

"Dill," he said, "I want to see you."

"What about?" I asked.

"Don't be a goof," he said nervously. "If I could tell you on the wire I wouldn't ask you up. It's not news. It's something you can do to save a guy from making a corpse of himself. Bill Latham told me you were a right guy and the one for the job. If he says so you're okay with me. How about it? Can you come over?"

I took a breath, "What've I got to lose? Where are you?"

"Forty-Fourth Street Hotel. Room 509. And make it snappy, Dill. This thing won't stand waiting."

"I am practically there," I said and hung up. The Old Man's eyes looked like a pair of traffic lights. He's got a nose like an anteater when it comes to scenting copy. I grinned at him. I remarked, "Ain't it awful how these dames keep chasing me?"

"There's no hayseed in this hair," he snapped, slapping the top of his bald head. "Who was it?"

"Uh-uh, temper! Mustn't!" I wagged my finger. "If anything develops you will read about it in due course. Meanwhile—" I picked up the handset again and I called Bill Latham, who runs the Hideaway Club between

Forty-Second and Forty-Third Streets, and who is a swell guy to boot.

I said, "Bill, Nicky Londo just called me and said he wanted to see me. He told me you suggested me. That on the level?"

Latham chuckled. "What's the matter, Daffy? Scared of Nicky?"

"Yea, verily," I said. "A reputation is a reputation and I value my young life."

"It's on the level," Latham said, laughing. "Londo called me about fifteen minutes ago. He said he had to get in touch with a right guy who was inside the law. He wouldn't tell me what for, said something about saving a screwy mug's life."

"Hokey," I replied. "That's all I wanted to know. See you when I'm thirsty, Bill. Thanks."

I hung up quickly, and before the Old Man could get his tongue going at me I skipped merrily out of his office, grabbed my coat and tore out through the reception office where platinum-haired Dinah Mason was sitting at her little table, directing the advertising traffic to and fro.

"Here's your hat. What's your hurry?" she clipped as I went by.

"Angel-Eyes," I said, "I'm getting up in the world. I am about to consort with a bumper-offer supreme and an income tax evader superb."

Dinah sniffed. "You and your screwy friends. Watch out that your nose stays clean, lunatic."

"Will you marry me?" I asked.

"That door you are about to depart through," she answered, "slams awfully easy. Be careful when you close it." And with that she handed me a Bronx plaudit which burned my ears.

I left and took a cab uptown.

2

MURDER BY REQUEST

NICKY LONDO WAS a giant. No kidding, he must have stood six feet four in his socks, and he carried plenty of weight on those big bones of his, not mentioning a very prodigious fallen chest where his belt went around the middle.

He awed me a little. He was black-haired, black-browed, and dark-eyed. It gave him a damned sinister aspect, especially the way his glimmers were stuck far back in their sockets above his oily, fat cheeks. But then I realized how nervous he was. That gave me the upper hand.

He had a smooth place in the hotel. A regular suite on the fifth floor, decked out with furniture and bric-a-brac which would have melted a connoisseur's heart.

When he motioned me to a smart modernistic sofa and lighted a cigarette for me I could see his pudgy hands shaking to beat the band. He sat down opposite me, lighting one himself. I could see he was trying to speak, but didn't know how to start.

I said, "All right, Nicky. Here I am. There you are. Lay the cards right down and get it off your mind."

"Okay," he said huskily. He leaned forward. "Do you know Gerald Mercer?"

"Mercer?" I muttered. "Gerald Mercer?" I snapped my fingers. "Why not? Gerald Mercer of Mercer & Garth? He's a partner in a brokerage office on the stock exchange."

"That's the one," said Londo. "What does he look like?"

"Nice-looking," I said, shrugging. "You know. Short, sort of. Wears a pince-nez. Gray-haired—nearly white, as a matter of fact. He wears a wing collar usually, with a speckled bow tie."

Londo sighed. "It's the same."

"What about him?" I asked. "Is he the one you said—"

Londo held up his hand. "I'll talk, Dill. You just listen. I wanted you here for two reasons. One—to see if maybe you could get this Mercer in an asylum where he belongs. Two—to clear me on this thing in case it goes through."

"I don't get you."

"You will." He jammed his cigarette into an ash tray and clenched his fists together. "This morning, around eight o'clock, the doorbell rings. I am shaving, it is so early. I go out to the door and this white-haired guy is standing there. He asks me if he can see me and he hands me his card. I see it is Gerald Mercer and I let him in. All the time, he is polite as hell. He hems and haws and finally gets around to what he came for. He says to me:

" 'How would you like to make fifty thousand dollars, Mr. Londo?'

" 'Well,' I says, 'that's a lot of coin. What's on your mind?' So he says:

" 'I'll pay you fifty thousand dollars if you will meet me tonight on the south end of the One Hundred and Twenty-Fifth Street Viaduct on Riverside Drive. All you have to do—after I hand you the case—is kill me.' "

I dropped my cigarette on the tray. "Wh-what?"

Londo waved his hand. "I'm only telling you what happened and it's all on the level."

I gulped. "Talk, friend. Keep talking."

"I figured he was nutty and that I'd better humor him. You know, I thought maybe he was having a nervous break-down or something, and that if I turned him away he might run into a guy who would really rub him out. Fifty grand is no chicken feed. Guys have murdered for less than that, you know."

"Me?" I said. "I don't know. That's your field."

He eyed me balefully. "Yeah. My field. That's why Mercer came to me first. He thought I was Number One knockoff man. I wish to hell the public would get rid of that idea!"

"After all—" I started.

He interrupted. "Listen, Dill. I'm no yokel. I made hay when the makings were good and I've got a cool million salted away. I'm out of the racket."

I grinned. "Nice going. But what about Mercer?"

Londo shrugged. "I told him I'd meet him. It's up to you now."

"Up to me?"

"Sure. To get in touch with him. Get in touch with his family. Put him in a nut-house. He's cracked."

I shook my head. "Sounds pretty screwy to me. Mercer sees you and offers fifty grand if you put the slug on him. If he wanted to die so bad, why didn't he commit suicide?"

"Because it wouldn't work out that way," said Londo.

"Workout?"

He flushed and set his jaw. "You know what I mean. I

asked him about that. He said no. Suicide was out. It had to be murder."

I'd caught Nicky at something and I didn't know what. His answer was lame.

"Hmm," I muttered.

"What did you say?"

"HMM," I ANSWERED. "Plain, common, ordinary 'hmm.' An exclamation indicating deep meditation. I was trying to understand what kind of reason a sane and sober gentleman like Gerald Mercer would have for wanting his life taken by a gunman—no offense." I sighed and got out of the chair. "Well, I'm always a sucker for riddles. I'll run down and either persade him he's batty or else I'll persuade a cop he is. It'll make a good feature anyway."

Londo frowned. "Do you have to write it with me in it?" he asked.

"Sure. That's my percentage."

"Well, guess you're right. I wish you wouldn't mention me, though. I don't like publicity." Not much he didn't! If he didn't really want me to write that yarn he'd have said so with a roscoe in my chest. There were angles in this thing. They bothered me almost as much as the hunches I began to get. I waved to him. "Hokey, Londo. I'm off to the races—"

The jingle of his telephone cut me off. He got up, a towering mass of flesh. "Wait and see. I'll see you to the door soon as I answer this."

He walked over to a side table next to the sofa where I'd been squatting and he picked up a neat job of a phone, a handset in bronze to match the heavy rug. He talked only a few seconds. I watched his face. It changed into what a thespian would call bafflement. "Okay," he said. "Okay by me, mister." And he hung up.

He stared at me. "Guess your trip is off, Dill."

"What?" I said. "I don't savvy."

"Your trip is off. Mercer's gotten smart."

I stopped ogling and pointed at the phone. "Was that he?"

Londo nodded. "He just said that the deal was off. He doesn't want to be killed anymore. He said it would be unnecessary now."

"Well, I'll be double-damned!" I snapped. "Thanks for a lot of trouble." I turned on my heel and went out the door, slamming it behind me as hard as I could.

In the corridor I didn't wait for the elevator. I found the exit staircase and went down it with rapidity which bid fair to sever my connections. When I reached the hotel lobby I grabbed occupancy of a public booth, painfully separated myself from a nickel, and called the *Chronicle*. I got Dinah.

"Listen, Gilded Lily," I said, "put this on a pad so's you can remember it and get it right. I want clippings from the morgue, savvy? The clippings and any other dope are to be on Gerald Mercer. 'M' as in mammy. 'E' as in eucalyptus. "R' as in—"

"The name," Dinah said dryly, "is Gerald Mercer. Got it the first time. Are you—"

Something happened at the other end. I heard a click. Then Dinah talked excitedly with some guy. She came back to yelp into the phone:

"Daffy, hold everything! The Old Man wants to talk with—"

She never even finished. The Old Man grabbed the phone out of her hand and bellowed, "Daffy!"

"My, what big tonsils you have," I said.

"Listen, you imitation pencil-pusher," the Old Man said in even, ominous tones, "I was just going by Dinah's desk when I heard her say, 'Gerald Mercer.' *What've you got?*"

I frowned. "What are you all excited about?" I asked. "I've just got a tip and a hunch. I wanted to check on Mercer's past life to see why he would hire a killer to bump him off."

"What?" The Old Man shrieked.

"Hey," I snapped. "Lay off that ear!"

"You damn fool! You damn fool!" he wailed. "If you got something, spill it! One of the biggest bits of industrial news just came through and you stand with your bare face hanging out!"

"Take it easy," I said, my voice taut. "Tell me, what's happened?"

"You know the firm of Mercer & Garth, stock brokers?"

"Yeah."

"They went under about an hour ago! Bankrupt! And one of the biggest scandals of the year! The firm was piffled out of six hundred thousand iron men. Six hundred grand embezzled! It was shaky enough with the market the way it is right now. And that six hundred Gs loss was enough to sink it!"

I whistled, hanging onto the phone. "Who heisted it?" I asked. "Who grabbed the six hundred grand?"

"Sherman Garth!" replied the Old Man lustily. "Garth, the partner of Mercer. He lifted the whole business!"

"Did they get him?"

There Was a pause at the other end.

"No."

"Why not?"

"He's dead. It was too much for him."

I tried to get my breath. "Too much for him? You mean he kicked himself in? Suicide?"

"You hit it. They find him in the washroom outside his office dead on the floor. He took cyanide and he left a note behind telling where the cash is! He put it in a safe deposit box under the name of John Mitchell in the Seacoast National Bank on Times Square. He left the keys with the note."

"Stand by," I said. "I'm on my way!"

3

THE CYANIDE PILL

LIEUTENANT BILL HANLEY of Inspector Halloran's more or less intelligent homicide squad looked sad when I came into the office of Mercer & Garth. "I thought so," he said. "Here we are having a nice, orderly investigation. Everybody was behaving except the corpse. Then from the depths of hell, you pop up."

"Why Poppa," I said, "how you do go on!"

Hanley smiled mysteriously. "What are you doing around, Daffy? Trying to make it a mystery?"

"Why not?" I said. "If I solve it, you might even get to be a captain."

"Sure," he said. "But the tough part is there's nothing to solve." There was a twinkle in his eyes. "I can read you, Daffy. You heard there'd been a suicide. You heard he took cyanide. Once you read somewhere how a famous dick solved a supposed cyanide suicide case when he discovered that the suicider had drunk the cyanide downstairs and died upstairs. Since cyanide works like lightning, it was plain to see that the suicider had been murdered."

I blushed redder than flannel underwear. I had been thinking along these lines. Hanley laughed uproariously. "I got you that time!"

"All right, wise guy," I said lamely. "Where's the corpse? Don't I get a look?"

Still laughing, he motioned me after him. We left the office and went down the corridor to the gentlemen's washroom. It was filled with police. A photographer was taking flashlight shots on all sides. Hanley elbowed his way through, with me in his shadow, and we reached the center of their attraction.

Sherman Garth was lying face down. He had been a tall man, with a face that emanated quiet dignity. His limp arms were buckled under his throat. Next to him on the floor, were pieces of shattered glass. His skin was cyanotic, quite different from the pallid waxiness of normal death. I sighed.

"He came in here after he wrote the letter," Poppa Hanley said. "Took a glass off that rack there. Dropped in the cyanide with some water and drank it. It got him before he could move. Glass broke. Chemical boys have most of it down at h.q. right now."

"Let's get out of here," I said.

We went out into the hall and walked back toward the office.

"Poppa, where's the letter he left?" I asked.

"Halloran has it," said Hanley, pulling his ear.

I looked surprised. "So the gorilla himself was here?"

Hanley nodded. "Why not? Embezzlement, firm failure, and suicide? Ain't that enough to bring out an inspector?"

"When you make jokes," I said, "Repugnant odors permeate the atmosphere. What was in the note?"

Hanley shrugged. "Nothing much. Garth admitted heisting around six hundred grand from the firm. Said he was going to lam, but he couldn't go through with it. Afraid of disgrace, he picked suicide. He left a key with the note and said the money would be found in safe deposit box at the Seacoast belonging to John Mitchell."

"Who's checking?"

"Inspector Halloran. He went down to the D.A.'s office to get an order permitting him to open the box. He should be over at the Seacoast right now. You didn't have an account with this firm, did you?"

"My young scallion," I said, "a Dill never gambles— in Wall Street stocks. Not since 1929 anyway. They took me for eighteen dollars in those days." I rubbed my nose. "Poppa."

"Yeah?"

"What about Garth? I don't like the look of the thing. What did he do all day? Did you check?"

"He came to business same as usual," Hanley replied. "Went through the morning and went out to lunch. It was right after he got back from lunch that he pulled the fadeout."

"Right after lunch!" I muttered. "I'd be damned if *I'd* commit suicide on a full stomach. I'd be so nervous I wouldn't have the strength to hold food down."

Hanley looked at me thoughtfully. "Yeah… that is a thought." He shrugged. "Oh, well, you can't always tell—"

"Where's Mercer?" I asked.

"In his office. He's all broken up. Looks like he knew the firm was on the rocks. He said he kind of thought that Garth was manipulating the books."

I grunted. "A ten-year-old could find six hundred Gs

manipulated, even if it was done in Burmese. What the hell kind of a business man was he, anyhow?"

"Garth's job was the books. Mercer had other work, he says."

"Let's see him." I smiled at Hanley. "I think maybe Gerald Mercer is going to prove very interesting when I bring up a little errand he was doing this morning."

Hanley looked suspicious. "What's this?"

"You'll see, Poppa."

WE WENT THROUGH the regular offices to the private office of Gerald Mercer, Hanley entered right in without knocking. Mercer was sitting behind his desk. He was smoking furiously. He looked pale as a sheet. He twitched, startled, when Hanley loomed in the doorway and said:

"Hello, Mr. Mercer. Boys treating you all right?" He meant Guilfoyle and Torrey, two homicide dicks who were sitting in the room with him.

"Very well, thank you," Mercer answered. He glanced at me. Hanley pointed at me. "This is Daffy Dill. The reporter. He said he wanted to see you."

"S-see me?" Mercer faltered. "I'm—terribly sorry. I can't possibly speak for the press. I'm in no condition—"

"Not for the press," I said. "Forget that. Just speak for the police."

Mercer rubbed his head. "I'm afraid I don't understand, Mr. Dill."

"Ever hear of a man named Nick Londo?" I asked.

He jerked. His eyes rose from the desk and stared into mine. It was a swell act. "So you know—"

Hanley, frowning, said, "What is this?"

"At eight this morning, this tomato saw Londo at the

Forty-Fourth Street Hotel and said he'd pay Londo fifty grand if Londo would bump him off."

Hanley jumped, his homely pan screwing into a beefy knot. "What did you say?"

"That's right, Mercer, isn't it?" I asked.

Mercer nodded and then heaved a sigh. "That's—right. I—I didn't think Londo would talk after I called the thing off—"

"You mean you asked Londo to—to kill you? You were willing to shell out fifty Gs to be murdered?" Hanley was aghast.

Mercer nodded nervously. "That's r-right, lieutenant."

"But in God's name, *why?*"

Mercer wet his lips. "It—it will sound fantastic in the papers. I suppose they'll brand me every kind of fool, perhaps call me mad. I—gentlemen, you can't understand. This firm was founded by my grandfather a—long time—ago." His voice caught. "And when I learned that Sherman had been stealing"— he paused to control himself—"stealing money which belonged to the firm's investors, and when I realized that by his thefts he had brought Mercer & Garth over the brim of financial failure—I just could not bear to think of the disgrace, the scandal, the dishonor which would have stigmatized the firm! All investors cheated out of their savings, their hard-earned money! It was unthinkable! This has always been an honest and honorable house, gentlemen. It was up to me—no matter what—to keep it that way."

"Go on," I said.

"I could not bring action against Sherman. He had been

my friend for—forty years." His voice fell to a whisper. "Forty years...."

There was a short silence. "I found only one thing to do. I was insured by the firm for five hundred thousand dollars double indemnity. This sum was payable only in the event that my death resulted from violence, with suicide excluded. I thought that if I could pay some one to—kill me—then the insurance would pay off the investors. Mercer & Garth would at least go down into dust in honor, not disgrace." He looked up, filmy-eyed. "Can you gentlemen understand a motive like that?"

"Sure," Hanley said. He looked all choked up as though he were going to bawl, He's a sentimental lug, anyway.

I said, "Where was the fifty grand pay-off coming from?"

"My personal estate."

"And how about Garth?" I asked. "Was he insured the same way? Does his death mean the investors will be paid?"

"He was not insured," Mercer said. "But thank God for the money he secreted in that box! That will even things up."

"And will the firm continue?"

Mercer shook his head sadly. "After a scandal like this?" He shrugged. "We could never get another client."

The telephone rang. Mercer reached for it, but Hanley got to it, first, saying, "I'll take it. Hello? Oh, hello, Chief!... What? No!... Well, I'll be—okay, okay, I will!" He hung up, chewing his lips; and glanced around the room at all of us.

"Mr. Mercer," he said finally, "I think your investors—"

"Wait a minute, Poppa," I said. "Let me guess at it. The investors are not going to get paid off because the mazuma—six hundred Gs in all—was *not* in the safe deposit box at the Seacoast National."

Hanley gasped. "How did you—"

"The hunch," I replied dulcetly, "is mightier than the clue."

4

DEATH AFTER LUNCH

MERCER ROSE SLOWLY from the desk, staring as he faced Hanley. "Is that true?" he asked, his voice taut.

Hanley nodded. "Afraid so, Mr. Mercer. That was Inspector Halloran on the phone."

"And was he sore!" I said.

"Yeah," said Hanley. "He was. He got the order from the D.A. all right, but all they found in the damn box was a savings bankbook with deposits totaling four grand. Not another thing."

"Then his note—" Mercer sank back. "He lied! Where is the money? Where is the six hundred—"

"I've got a pretty good idea," I said, watching the ceiling. And as Poppa Hanley opened his mouth to query, I added, "But since newspaper men are not compelled to divulge info sources, I think I'll keep it to myself for awhile. Poppa, here's one of your henchmen. He's found something."

It was a third-class dick named Fogarty. He had that leering, self-satisfied expression on his pan which indicated that he was better than h.q. rated him, and that he had just made the most important discovery (maybe) in the case. Hanley snapped, "Well?"

"Look," said Fogarty. He held out a little box. "Pills,

Chief. A box full of 'em. Now I gotta theory that this guy, Garth, he took one of these pills and it had cyanide in it, see?"

"Oh, nonsense!" Mercer murmured. "Those were Sherman's indigestion pills. He always took one now and then."

"Let's see them, Poppa," I said. He handed me the box. There was a sort of prescription on the outside. It read: *"One or two capsules to be taken after each meal."*

I gave the box back to Poppa, who handed it to Fogarty. "All right, Sherlock," Hanley said. "Suppose you take these down to headquarters and have the chem boys give them a going over." Poppa was ribbing the guy. He knew as well as I did that those pills were harmless. Fogarty didn't like the idea of removing his brains from the scene of the holocaust, but he'd asked for the long walk and so he left for Centre Street.

I'd seen enough and it appeared to me that the time had come to break the case wide open. There was no telling when the boys might take it on the lam, carrying the six hundred Gs along with them. And that was too much mazuma to take chances with.

As I said, Hanley knew as well as I did that those pills were harmless. But for different reasons. Hanley figured that if Garth committed suicide, he would have used ordinary cyanide tablets without any hocus-pocus about sticking the stuff in indigestion pills. My hunch was that if Garth had been murdered and the cyanide *had* been given via the pills, there had certainly been a switch in pill boxes by the time the police were warming their heels at the *situs criminis.*

I was up on Poppa one point, you see. I knew that Sherman Garth had been bumped off—and not by his own hand.

It's queer how little things can change the whole aspect of a case. Not liking it much, I was nevertheless willing to string along with the suicide theory, despite the missing money, which should have been in that safe deposit box.

But when I heard one thing, it didn't make the suicide jell. A guy who's about to kill himself doesn't consider the job so calmly and so coolly that he goes out to lunch just before swallowing the bad news.

Sherman Garth had eaten lunch ten minutes before he died. I thought to myself, being my best friend: Daffy—suppose you had wheedled six hundred thousand dollars out of Mercer & Garth. Suppose when the time came for the runout powder with the mazuma, you lost your nerve and couldn't go through with it. Suppose you were so upset, that your conscience bothered you so much, you forced yourself to sit down, write a true confession, and then to swallow some delectable cyanide of potassium. I ask you, comrade, would you have put away a slice of ham and a couple of genuine eggs ten minutes before the passout, with maybe a dish of raspberry sherbet on the side?

Uh-uh.

A conscience which is so finicky that it puts a guy in his grave doesn't let him eat a hearty meal before the climax.

I LEFT POPPA Hanley, the office boys, and Gerald Mercer, after a lot of verbal barrages and I took the elevated down to Wall Street. I looked around, found a drug store and went in. Yassuh, there was a public booth there. I called the Old Man.

"Listen, Horace Greeley," I said, "break down the front page and dust off your black type."

He snapped, "What's coming?"

"The Mercer & Garth story."

"Front page?" he said. "That's no screamer yarn. It's hot for the market page, but a suicide is a sui—"

"Wait a sec'," I said. "Did I say suicide?"

"Sure. Sherman Garth. You got the dope, didn't you?"

"The dope?" I said. "You put it mildly, my man. I beg to inform you and your imitation newspaper that Sherman Garth was murdered."

The Old Man screamed, "What?"

"My goodness, what a voice," I said.

There was a pause. When the Old Man spoke again, he was his old calculating self. "I'll break the front page down, Daffy. Do the police know yet?" He held his voice down, soft and low.

"Not an inkling."

"You're sure?"

"As sure as I ever was."

"Good. Now listen. Can you break it for the Wall Street Closing edition?"

"I get it," I said. "You want it to tie up with your financial section, too." I glanced at a clock over the soda counter in the drug store. "That only gives me twenty minutes to deadline."

"Well?"

I sighed. "Okay, slave-driver. Twenty minutes and the yarn breaks. Hold onto your hat and tell Louie to write me a nice obit and tell Dinah I died with her name on my lips." I hung up.

Immediately, I pulled out the directory and looked up the number of the Forty-fourth Street Hotel. When I found it, I also found another nickel in my jeans—deep down—and I dropped it in the coin slot and called the number. When I got the hotel, I said, "Nicky Londo's suite, please."

There was a click. While they were buzzing him, I pulled out a handkerchief and spread it over the mouthpiece. I had just finished, when a voice said huskily, "Londo."

"Th-this is M-Mercer," I faltered, turning on the talent which had made me the leading ham thespian in Punxatawney (Pa.) chautauquas.

Londo's breath whistled on the intake. "You fool—why call here?"

"I—I had to," I whined. "I can't stand it any more. I c-can't. The way—he—looked when they found him— I can't! Do you hear me! I'm going to tell! I can't stand this!"

"Mercer!" Nicky Londo's voice was still husky, but he gave it a penetrating vibrance which made me shiver.

"Y-yes?" I said.

"Take hold of yourself. Listen to me. Where are you?"

"At m-my apartment."

"Police with you?"

"No. Alone. I left them at the office. They were hounding me."

"Sure you weren't tailed?"

"Absolutely."

"Okay." Londo drew a breath. "Now, listen, Mercer, there's nothing to get afraid of. Nobody can pin anything on you. You're clear. Now you just wait there at your apartment for me. I'm coming over."

"All right," I said. "B-but hurry. I'm afraid…."

I hung up. I stared at the mouthpiece for a second. It had worked. And Nicky Londo, probably as jittery as a hula dancer that Mercer would sing, was on his way to Mercer's home spot to put the slug on the cohort in crime!

There wasn't any time to lose. I fished out the third and last nickel, dropped it in the slot, and left the handkerchief over the mouthpiece while I called the offices of Mercer & Garth.

"I want to speak with Mr. Mercer," I said huskily. I swear I sounded more like Londo than he did himself.

"Hello?"

"Mercer? This is Londo. Can you talk?"

"No," Mercer snapped. "Not now. We are handling no more stock orders at this firm. Sorry."

"I get it," I said, still huskily. "But don't hang up, guy. Something's gone wrong, see? Nothing serious. It can be fixed. But I got to see you right away. I'm going up to your apartment. Meet me there in ten minutes or I'll spill the beans. I know the bulls are there. Get away from there and them. Your apartment. And don't be tailed."

"V-very well," Mercer said nervously. He hung up.

"Ah me!" I sighed, sticking my handkerchief back into my pocket. I left the drug store after looking up Mercer's residence, which was located in one of the remodeled houses over on Sutton Place.

There was a red hack at the curb. The driver had a pan that only a mother could love. He grinned at me. "Taxi, mister?"

I took out a nice crisp fin and waved it under his nose.

"No kidding," he said. "Is it real? I haven't seen five bucks since that newsreel where they burned the old ones in Washington."

"My friend," I said, "it's yours if you and me and this can you call an automobile can get to Sutton Place in any time under ten minutes."

"Brother," he said, "I just earned it. Don't close that door too tight. You'll be opening it again by the time you sit down."

5

—

DEADLINE

HE DAMNED NEAR did just that. I hadn't even finished my cigarette when he slammed on the brakes and skidded dexterously against the curb in front of Gerald Mercer's apartment house—Clayborn Arms, as I recall.

I tossed the cigarette away and got out of the car. I snapped my fingers. "Damn!"

The driver frowned. "Forget something, boss?"

"I'll say I did, Pegasus," I replied. I squinted at him. "You wouldn't happen to be the proud owner of a rod at the moment, would you?"

He looked at me soberly. "You a dick?"

"No," I said. "Are my feet that flat? I'm Daffy Dill."

"The news guy?"

"You called it, friend. How about it—don't tell me you really have a gun!"

He nodded and beckoned me over. It was in the side pocket of the cab. "Sometimes I might need it," he said. "Stickups happen all around this town. But I gotta be careful. I don't have a permit. You on a case, boss? That why you want it?"

"Pegasus," I said, "I am about to snare two boys who

would rather kill than eat. And I hate doing it with my bare hands."

"Gee!" He looked wide-eyed. "Here. You can have it." He pulled it out and slipped it to me. "Watch yourself. There's only one pill in it. I don't have any more. How long—"

"You wait down the block," I said. "I'll need you in about fifteen minutes."

He nodded. "Okay, boss. Good luck. Gee!"

As he drove off, I went in. It was a regular apartment. I buzzed some one else's doorbell so's they'd tick to let me past the downstairs door. I got inside the hall and caught my bearings. Looking at every door, I started upstairs, trying to locate Mercer's.

I finally found it on the third. I went half way up the stairs to the fourth floor and sat down on the steps, where I could watch that door.

I waited there about four minutes when heavy steps came up the stairs. I hunched down, breathlessly. Sure enough, big Nicky Londo came into sight through the bannister spokes. I gulped, seeing how grim and set his face was. He glanced around carefully. I took a quick look at the rod I'd gotten from the cabby. My God, it was a .22 target pistol! And he said there was only one slug in it. A hell of a lot of good a .22 was going to do unless I clipped someone in the head with it.

Londo took out a key and opened Mercer's door. He went right in and slammed it behind him. I noticed he had gloves on. He was set for a job, right enough.

I waited....

Not more than five minutes later, the automatic self-op-erating elevator whirred. I had a hunch that Mercer was due. The elevator stopped at the floor and he got out. He looked pale. His hands were trembling slightly as he pushed a key in the lock and opened the door.

It closed after him gently, leaving me alone in the hall.

I got up, came to the third floor and went to the window just opposite the elevator. It opened onto a fire escape which also fronted Mercer's bedroom, as I found out when I climbed outside on it. The bedroom window was unlocked and half open.

I slid it quietly up the rest of the way. Their voices reached me. I crouched on the fire escape. I could look into the living room through the gap between some coppery drapes.

"*I* phoned you?" Mercer snapped. "You're mad! I couldn't phone you. I was at the office with police all around. *You* phoned *me* and told me to meet you here! What are you trying to pull?"

Londo was sitting in a chair directly opposite me. His eyes were slits as they watched Mercer's every movement beadily. Mercer was directly in front of me with his back turned toward me as he faced Londo.

Londo said in a purr, "Mercer, either you phoned me or someone else is in on the set-up. I think the set-up is okay. I don't think anyone has tumbled. And what I want to know is—why did you call if you say everything is going smoothly? Figuring a double-cross?"

"Why, you rat—" Mercer snapped. It looked funny, him saying that to Londo who was twice his size. He took a step forward and waved his hand under Londo's nose. "I didn't call you. And that's the truth!"

Londo smiled easily. "Okay, if that's the way you play. Okay with me." He reached his hand into his pocket and slowly pulled out a pistol. It was a big, glistening black thing with a thin, long barrel. He said softly: "Stand still, Mercer. We're going to part ways. I can't trust a liar."

Mercer gaped. "For God's sake—"

"Skip it," Londo said. Holding the gun on Mercer's belly, he slowly got up and walked across to the grand piano, where he yanked a beautiful Spanish shawl off the top and wrapped it securely around the muzzle of the gun. It must have made six layers and it was a cinch to muffle the shot. My gag had worked well. I figured if I got them leery of each other, they might spill the beans.

Mercer couldn't say a word. He was trapped. His eyes showed it.

Londo nodded to him. "Six hundred Gs goes a long way for a single guy. I guess you were figuring it like that yourself. Planned to get me over here and bump me off with one of those nice little cyanide tablets. Come clean now. Didn't you?"

"No!" Mercer whispered. "Listen, Londo, I didn't—"

"Skip it," Londo said grimly. "Where's the pills?"

MERCER'S HAND DUG down into his vest pocket. It came out holding a little box which was identical with the one Fogarty had unearthed in Sherman Garth's desk at the Mercer & Garth offices.

Londo took the box and slipped it in his pocket. "Did you work the switch all right?"

Mercer nodded, owl-eyed with terror. "After he took a pill and went to the washroom, I put this box in my pocket and put the original back in his desk... Listen, Londo—"

"Where's your key?"

"Wh-what?" Mercer gasped.

"Your key. I want your key to the box. Or do you want me to find it myself after I shoot you?"

Mercer dug into his vest again, this time bringing out a small key which he handed to Londo.

That was enough. I stepped into the apartment and crossed to the drapes and I snapped, "Hold it, gents! The play is over!"

They wheeled and ogled at me, the blood draining from their faces. When they believed their eyes, they both looked at one another and comprehension pervaded their faces.

"Framed!" Mercer rasped.

"Framed!" snapped Londo. "Dill called you! Dill called me!"

"And Dill now calls both of you guys to lay down your arms and disperse, ye rebels," I said. "Up with your paws, Londo, and drop that rod!"

Londo shrugged. "Sure, Dill. It's your show."

Which went to show what a sucker I was for my ability to awe people. I thought the sight of me and the sight of the nice lethal rod in my hand would make Londo awed enough to quit. What a laugh. I awed him about as much as a flea awes an elephant.

He half turned as though to lay the pistol on top of the desk where Mercer still sat. Then he grunted.

Next thing I knew, Londo was down behind the desk and orange flame was being fanned across the room, intermingling with the ominous drone of freed bullets.

I really saw him dive for the cover of the desk and I had a chance for a shot at him. But I held on. With one slug in the .22 I didn't want to try it out in a snap shot at a moving target.

The bullets from Londo's gun hit the wall on my right side with thuds as heavy as hammers. I fell backwards into the bedroom, and I let out a yell like a banshee.

Simultaneously, I laid down on the bedroom floor with my head peering around the corner of the door *beneath* the fringy end of the copper drapes and I drew a bead on the top of the desk where the stabs of gun-flame had come from.

The tortured yell brought Londo's head and gun up curiously. He hadn't expected to hit me in the wild fusillade which he let go and the fact that he had—so he thought from my cry of pain—surprised him.

When his whole head was over the rim of the desk, I pulled the trigger.

For a second, when the .22 barked like a lapdog and did a neat little jump of recoil, I couldn't see him through the white smoke.

It cleared. His head was still over the rim. But his eyes were closed and there was a black spot where his nose met his forehead. Even as I watched him, gritting my teeth as blood started to trickle down his cheeks, he slowly relaxed and tumbled behind the desk.

I went to my feet and ran like hell into the living room to get hold of Londo's rod before Mercer, who had sat at the desk through it all like a dazed hypnotic, got any ideas.

It was as though he caught the thought through mental telepathy. He took one look at my flying frame and he wrapped himself around the big rod before I had a chance to get within five feet of the desk.

"Stand still," he snapped.

HE DIDN'T FIRE. He didn't have the nerve to fire because I

was still holding the .22, which he didn't know was empty. But he held the gun on me, trying to think what he would do. He was thinking fast. His eyes went back and forth to Londo, to me, to Londo again.

Something cracked! It came from the bedroom. I recognized the fire of a .38 and I saw Londo's gun sail out of Mercer's hand and travel clear across to the opposite wall. I dove for it and had it in my paw before it even bounced.

I turned. Mercer was sitting at the desk, wailing furiously while he wrung a shocked hand. There was a man standing in the bedroom doorway, a man in a gray topcoat and a gray fedora hat, whose pan was homely but honest. I said:

"Hello, Poppa."

Hanley shook his head. "Some day, Daffy, you're gonna get yourself killed, pulling tricks like this without telling me. Why didn't you take him?"

"With this?" I held up the .22 and shook my head. "It didn't have a bullet in its bosom. How'd you stumble in on crime?"

Hanley looked serious. "I'm not as dumb as I look, Daffy. I tailed this guy Mercer when he left the office after that phone call. I had an idea you made the call. It's like you to get the hell off the scene in a hurry and then cook up something. You cluck, you might've gotten yourself killed and made more trouble for me. How did these guys do it?"

I glanced at Mercer. "How about it, poisoner?"

Mercer's head drooped. He sighed. "I'll talk, gentlemen."

Well, he told it just the way you read it in the *Chronicle*. Londo had lost a lot of money on the market through Mercer & Garth, Inc. He was nearly broke. The firm itself was shaky. It was operating on a surplus left over from the "good ole days." Mercer and Londo got together. They filched the firm of the surplus—six hundred grand—and then they pulled that stunt about Mercer trying to get killed.

The idea of the thing was to work up sympathy for Mercer as the sacrificing honest member of the firm. This was to help clear him when Garth supposedly committed suicide. What Mercer did was to substitute cyanide for indigestion pills when Garth went out to lunch, and to switch boxes again after Garth died.

The cash we found in a joint safe deposit box in the Cornwall Exchange on Broad Street. The names were Mark Cain and Louis Harris. Both of the guys, Londo and Mercer, had to be present with their keys in order to open up the box.

And I still have to smile when I think of Londo that morning telling me, "I'm no yokel. I've put away over a cool million." Yah! He had like hell!

Later, the Old Man told me:

"You see, Daffy? Just like I said. When a dog bites a man, that's routine. When a man bites a dog, that's news!"

"So it is, so it is," I said. "But what the devil has that to do with this case?"

The Old Man sighed. "Don't you see? When a gunman shoots a guy, that's routine. But when a guy *asks* a gunman to shoot him, that's—"

"Holy, holy, holy!" I said. "How about a raise?"

Anyway, he gave me a day off.

GREEN MAMBA

Every Clue Daffy Dill Unearths Is Front Page News in the Amazing Mystery of the Dead Oil King and the Lost Snake

1

SNAKE MISSING!

IT WAS NINE-THIRTY A.M. when my telephone brought me reluctantly out of a sound sleep. I yawned once and picked up the handset and said, "Hello?"

"Daffy," said the Old Man at the *Chronicle*, "I've got a story for you."

"Thanks so much," I said, "but I can do without it."

"I thought it might appeal to your herpetological side. There's a snake missing."

"A what?"

"A snake, serpent, reptile. A.W.O.L. Missing."

I said sadly, "You don't want me. You want the Zoo."

"You'll do," the Old Man replied dryly. "It's a green mamba. A guy named Professor Anton Goetel telephoned police headquarters about fifteen minutes ago and said it had escaped from his serpentarium. He wanted a radio alarm broadcast. He said it was poisonous."

"He put it mildly," I said. "The green mamba happens to be the fastest snake alive and the second deadliest to populate this cruel world of ours. I suppose you had some idea of getting me out to bring it back alive for the sake of the *Chronicle's* circulation?"

He grunted. "That's right"

*Into the room stepped
John Boyle*

"Well, Rasputin, when it comes to capturing green mambas alive, I simultaneously announce my resignation from the Fourth Estate."

"Listen, Daffy," the Old Man said cuttingly, "you're getting to be a sissy. You're losing your umph. You haven't turned in an exclusive beat for two weeks... Are you slipping?"

"Like a suction-cup," I snapped. "Okay, slave-driver, I'm a sucker for your slurs. Who is this Goetel bird who owns the thing?"

"He's a professor of toxicology at Columbia University. Supposed to be a super-whiz on all kinds of poisons and stuff and things. I just looked up all the data on him that we had in the morgue. His specialty is snakes. He's been working on an ultra-violet radiation principle, which is meant to detoxify venoms... I dunno. He sounds kind of screwy to me. He has a regular hothouse snake den in his back yard with reptiles from all over the world in it."

"Anything else?"

"Yeah. He's got a son. William Goetel. The boy is twenty-three and a swell snake-man himself. Following in father's footsteps, as it were. He goes to Columbia as a student. He graduates this June."

"And when Goetel found this green mamba missing, he buzzed h.q. for an alarm?"

"That's right. How about it, scribe?"

I said, "I'll cover, chief," and I hung up.

I was in the middle of a hasty shave when the telephone rang again.

It was a girl. She said: "I want to speak with Daffy Dill!"

She had a contralto voice, soft and husky, and—at the moment—excitedly breathless. She was refined and cultured. I could tell by the precise way she slung her words. I said, "Speaking."

"The reporter?"

"The *Chronicle's* claim to fame," I said.

"I had to be certain," she said warily, "You're the one who helped out Clare Gordon that time she was kidnaped?"

"The same," I said. "What's on your mind, lady?"

"I want help," she replied sharply. "There's been a murder. William Goetel, my fiancé, will probably be arrested for it. But he didn't do it! I know he didn't! And I want you to prove it!"

"Whoa!" I said, feeling a scoop hovering somewhere in the vicinity. "Who are you, anyway?"

"My name—is Rina LeBreque."

"Not the Rina LeBreque," I remarked, awed, "who is the filly of one Roger LeBreque, a gentleman who is said to own the half of Oklahoma where the oil wells are?"

"Yes, yes, that's it! Will you help me? I'll—I'll pay you a thousand dollars if you can prove that William Goetel did not do it."

"Sure, I'm on," I said. "But where are you, and who's dead?"

There was no answer.

The wire was dead. I pressed down the hook a few times and got the operator. "Sorry, sir," she said. "Your party hung up."

I PUT THE handset back on the prong and I looked up the telephone number of the LeBreque mansion on Riverside Drive and 77th Street. Oddly enough, this spot was a mere block away from where the missing green mamba had previously resided. I called the place and was rewarded with a gruff reply from a guy I knew. "Yeah?"

"The name is Daffy Dill, Inspector Halloran. I would like to speak with a girl named Rina."

"She ain't talking to no one."

"She just talked to me," I said.

"We were cut off."

"What are you trying to pull? She ain't talked to nobody for the last twenty minutes. She's right where I can keep an eye on her. Now you cut it out, Daffy, or I'll really get sore!"

Halloran slammed down on the other end with a crash that played chopsticks on my ear-drums. I shrugged and called the *Chronicle*. Dinah Mason answered and put me through to the Old Man.

I said, "Listen, chief. Have you had any word from the police reporters on Halloran's whereabouts?"

"Not a word. Why?"

"Because he's at the home of Roger LeBreque, the oil king."

"It's murder," the Old Man breathed. "It's murder if Halloran is there. And a big one at that!

"And listen," I said, "I think a murder and the missing snake tie up."

The Old Man choked. "Daffy—so help me—if you give me heart failure like this and nothing pans out—"

I said, "Be yourself! I'm covering. Keep the forms open, and tell Sampson to meet me at the LeBreque house."

2

ONE FANG

I DIDN'T GO to the LeBreque place right off. Instead, I dropped in on Professor Anton Goetel, who lived on West 78th Street, directly behind LeBreque. In fact, their back yards connected, unfenced.

Goetel was a frowzy old bird with gray sideburns and a bald head. He wore cheaters and had an absentminded face. He was nice enough about everything, and he took me into his back yard where the snake-house was.

It was a sight to behold. It resembled a hothouse, all glass-paned and shining. He unlocked the door and we went in. Three-quarters of the place was lined with snake dens. Each den had glass sides and was covered on top with a thin wire meshing. Rattlers, coral snakes, moccasins, cobras, adders, three green mambas, and even a couple of Gila monsters... Just a nice old home week.

The rest of the joint was strictly laboratory. There were shelves with test tube racks and test tubes, all filled with greenish-yellow stuff. Professor Goetel pointed all the works out to me and finally wound up in front of the mamba den, saying:

"Here was where I had the missing *Dendrascips* specimen. There were four in all, you see... Walter LeBreque brought them back from the Congo for me...."

"Walter LeBreque?" I echoed.

"Why, yes," the professor said, mildly surprised. "Do you know him too? He lives right behind me."

"I thought Roger LeBreque owned that place," I said.

Goetel nodded absently. "So he does. Walter is his younger brother." He looked apologetic. "Walter's rather the black sheep of the family, you know. Always wanting to get away and explore. He went to Africa on this last trip. Got back two weeks ago. He promised to bring me some mambas and he did—four of them."

"When did you find the snake missing?"

"About eight-thirty this morning... That is—yes. Eight-thirty. I came out for my notes for class—or was it—no, that's right. And when I got here, the mamba was gone. I was terribly upset—first time I missed classes since my sister's funeral four years ago—"

"I understand," I said. "But how did the beastie get away?"

He leaned down. "See here—this wire mesh has been pried up a trifle. Not much, just a trifle. Snakes do that by constant rubbing. And see here—one of the panes of glass in this serpentarium is broken. An accident last week. The snake glided to freedom through there."

"How long would it take a snake to push up wire by rubbing?"

"They do it all the time. A month, perhaps." He rubbed his chin and stared vaguely around the place. "I do wish I could find that tube—"

This gink was beginning to get me. He was so absentminded. I entertained grave fears that the missing mamba might be in his vest pocket. I said anxiously, "Something else missing?"

"No," he said slowly. "It—er—really isn't missing—"

"What?"

"Why—" he adjusted his spectacles—"there's a test tube of Gaboon viper venom gone from its rack. I'm sure I must have mislaid if around here somewhere."

I took one look at the squalid Gaboon viper with the maple-leaf head and I turned icy. "Proffy, with a memory like that, you're Public Enemy Number One. That stuff is deadly, isn't it?"

"Oh, very!"

"And you don't know where it is?"

"It's around… somewhere…."

I gulped and took a good look around. "Proffy, you've got an offspring. Where is he?"

"He's out of town. I really don't know where. He got a telephone call this morning and left rather hurriedly… He said he would get in touch with me later. I do wish I could remember where I put that tube of venom—"

"Whoa," I said. "Lemme out of here before I need a shot of antivenin!"

I went down to 77th Street where I found a burly flat-foot standing in front of the gray-stone LeBreque mansion, meaningly swinging a nightstick in his paw. He didn't faze me. I flashed the tin pawnshop badge I carry behind my lapel and I snapped, "Holmes is the handle. I'm from the homicide bureau. Halloran sent for me."

"Scram," he said. "Halloran told me to be on the lookout for that Sherlock Holmes gag and Daffy Dill. Beat it before I run you in for impersonating an officer."

"Why," I said, thinking of Halloran. "The dirty so-and-so!"

I went around on Riverside Drive. The west side of the LeBreque house ran along the Drive for half a block. I took a good look at the stones. They had enough crevices for a foothold if the vines would hold my weight. I tried the vines. No dice. They were too weak. They wouldn't hold me. And right then and there, I lost my breath.

I'D FOUND SOMETHING. There was a stout manila rope behind those vines and it went up to the open window on the second floor!

Throwing caution to the winds, I climbed up, and when I laid my panting chin across the window-sill on the second floor, somebody gasped, "Well, for gos'sakes!" and pulled me into the room bodily.

It was Bill Hanley, chewing on a dry, unlighted cigar, and looking very much agape.

"Hello, Poppa. Surprised?" I said.

"Hell," he grunted. "You couldn't surprise me if you flew in here on your own wings. But that rope—"

"Trust a Dill," I said, "to unearth a clue. Yes, indeed, Poppa, when it comes to—" I stopped abruptly. The room was a bedroom.

In the bed—the cause of my loss of speech—reposed Roger LeBreque....

I never want to see a corpse like that again.

The muscles of LeBreque's face had contorted horribly. The snarling lips were deep purple. Both of his hands were bunched into fists and were reaching toward his throat. His pajama shirt was ripped wide open from the chaos of death.

His hair had been snow-white. Against the blackened hue of his flesh, the contrast was grisly. A yellow ray of sunlight played across his bared teeth. He was all out of shape, badly swollen. His open eyes were widely dilated.

But the ghastly part of the thing was the blood. Blood all over the place. His eyes, his nose, his ears, his mouth, anything that could bleed, had bled.

I said, "Poppa, that's awful!"

"What happened?"

"We got the call at about eight o'clock through telegraph bureau. We came right up. That's the way we found him. We've been checking this room. Halloran has the boys and girls on the carpet downstairs."

"Was the Vulture here?" I asked. The "Vulture" is Dr. Kerr Kyne, chief medical examiner. Hanley nodded. "What'd he say?"

Hanley pointed down at the dead man's chest. "Right there—over the heart."

I looked. There was a single flaming dot in the black flesh. It was raw and angry. The entire toxic condition seemed to centralize at that one point. "Well?"

"Snake-bite," Hanley said. "Kyne says a poisonous snake bit him. What do you think of that?"

I nearly fainted. "What are you standing here for?" I yelped. "Don't you know? Haven't you heard?"

"What's the beef?"

"Somebody stole a green mamba out of a snake den behind LeBreque's property sometime last night! A guy named Goetel owns it! He called the cops this morning! Didn't you hear?"

"No!" Hanley boomed, brightening. "You don't say! Stolen?"

"Of course it was! Goetel thought it had escaped, but the cluck told me it took a month for a snake to pry up the wire mesh on top of the den and he'd only had this mamba for the last two weeks!"

"Swell," Hanley said with enthusiasm. "Come on downstairs. I'll tell Halloran."

"Hold it a second," I said. "Something's phony. Something is plenty phony!" I stared at the corpse and then at him. "What about that rope? Was there a heister in here last night?"

Hanley pointed at the desk. "Daffy, the door to this room was locked on the inside last night. And on that desk we found a full print of a left hand."

"Where is it?"

"Babcock took it down to h.q. to check it."

"Would a professional crook leave a handprint?"

Hanley shook his head. "But it kinda looked as though he was scared into grabbing the desk. I figured whoever it was, saw the murder done, and was panicked into holding the desk for support. Anyway, that door has a snap-lock. Once the door is closed, it locks inside. No one tinkered with it. LeBreque's secretary, John Boyle, had the key. So the crook came through the window. That's why the rope."

"But why isn't the hand-print Boyle's or someone else's in the house?"

"Because this heister used a chisel on these desk drawers.

See there? But he never finished the job. He was scared off. Now what in hell is so phony?"

"That," I said. I pointed at the livid dot over Roger LeBreque's heart. Hanley frowned furiously.

"How come?"

"Snakes have two fangs," I said. "Was this green mamba an exception to the rule? Where's the mark of the other fang? There isn't any!"

Hanley just looked at me dumbly. He didn't know the answer.

3

AN ARREST

BUT IN THE upper hall, I picked up the telephone while Bill Hanley went downstairs. "Listen, Poppa," I told him, "you tell that Rina LeBreque dame to meet me at the foot of the stairs. I crave to sling words with her privately."

"Okay," Hanley said. "Hurry up."

I called the *Chronicle* and got the Old Man. I said, "See if you can wrap your brains around this one, Rasputin. I want effects."

"What kind of effects?"

"I want the effect of green mamba venom on the human body," I said. "And then I want the effect of Gaboon viper venom on the same. Can you get that straight, with your crooked mind?"

"I can," the Old Man sighed. "What's happened?"

"News," I said. "Give me Brad for rewrite."

I gave Brad the entire yarn as far as it had gone, slipped a "more to come" tag on the end, and then went downstairs.

Rina LeBreque was standing at the foot of the stairs. She was tall and dark and she had a jaw that told me she knew her way around. Her eyes were decidedly hostile and suspicious as she looked me over.

I said in a low voice, "I'm Daffy Dill."

She stared at me. She said coldly, "Really? What am I supposed to do—swoon or cheer?"

That stopped me. "Why the whiff of Iceland, lady? Why'd you call me in the first place?"

She met my eyes and said evenly, "Are you insane? I haven't the slightest idea what you're talking about."

I groaned. I had expected this. "Something's phony," I said. "This is the phoniest case I ever did see…" We went back to the living room. Halloran was standing in the center of the room, loudly berating every one.

There was a white-haired old dame with an evil eye and a stout cane. Her chin was out and every now and then she'd throw a beautiful crack at Halloran about his lack of mentality. She was Agatha LeBreque, a maiden of sixty-five years, Roger LeBreque's elder sister.

That stuff about an evil eye was no joke. Her left eye was blue, and as cold and glassy as pure crystal. It never moved, just fixed on you and stayed there. It gave me the jitters.

Besides Rina, there was another girl. Her name was Alison LeBreque. She had ash-blond hair and timid gray eyes. She cringed away from Inspector Halloran's imitation of an inspector. She was Walter LeBreque's daughter, Roger's niece.

Walter LeBreque was next, a big man with a bronzed skin, roughened from the tropics. He was strong as an ox. His cheeks were quivering as he sat beside Agatha on the sofa. His act was good.

Then there was the little man, John Boyle, who was pretty ordinary-looking. Quiet, almost sissified, he wore a quiet suit with several sharpened lead pencils sticking out of his upper left coat pocket. He was around thirty years old, but the kind of egg who ages before his time from pure preciseness. He'd been the dead man's secretary.

The last and sixth person was a big, corpulent individual who puffed on a cigar and kept muttering, "Outrageous! Some one shall certainly hear of this!" He was Dr. Marvin McKay, LeBreque's personal sawbones. He looked like a traveling salesman.

Bill Hanley told Halloran about the missing mamba and the Inspector nearly detonated. He started to rave excitedly and he wound up with:

"—getting someplace! So that was it! You watch these killers, Hanley! Claghorn and me are going over to Goetel's!" He breezed out.

The room was very quiet. I told Hanley about the phony call I had had that morning. He said aloud, "But if Rina didn't phone you, then who did?"

"I don't believe anyone did." Rina sneered.

"Pardon me, Mrs. Astorbilt," I said, "but you are in error. And if you want to play rough, I'll go further. The point of the call was this: When whoever phoned knew about the murder and heard Dr. Kyne give a verdict of death by snake-bite, that person immediately felt that William Goetel, being an expert snake-man, would be arrested for the killing... How'm I doing, Poppa?"

Rina smiled coldly. "I think," she said, "I can help you out."

"Yeah?"

"THE PERSON WHO called you was my esteemed cousin, Alison. She is the only one who might be affected by William Goetel's implication. They're in love. She probably was afraid to use her own name. She's so timid, you know!"

Alison leaped to her feet. "That isn't so! That isn't why I used it!" Her voice was contralto, soft and husky.

"That's the voice," I said. "Explain, lady."

"I wanted you to help me out. I didn't think you'd—do it for nothing. I thought if I said I was Rina and offered you a thousand dollars you might get interested. Later I was going to explain to you. I didn't have the money myself, and the inspector nearly caught me calling and I had to hang up on you."

Hanley frowned. "Well, Daffy?"

"Sounds kosher, Poppa," I said. "If she's got a logical reason why young Goetel might have been suspected of killing Roger LeBreque—"

John Boyle stirred uneasily. "I think I can explain that," he said hesitantly. "I was with Mr. LeBreque when he had the scene with Mr. Goetel. He disliked the boy intensely. He threatened to disinherit Miss Alison if they married. But, of course, Mr. Goetel would never have done murder to gain his ends. He was too nice a boy. He'd have married Miss Alison and told Mr. LeBreque to go to the devil."

Alison was on the sofa, shedding tears like Pago-Pago in the rainy season. Her father had his arm around her. I started to ask her a question when Dr. McKay spluttered, "Don't bother the girl, Dill! Can't you see she's distraught?"

"Okay," Hanley said dryly. "Maybe you'll tell me what you're doing over here."

Dr. McKay gave him a dirty look. "None of your insolence, sir. I know my rights. Ahum." He swelled like a balloon. "The truth of the matter is I came to report a loss. Ahum. I am missing a twenty-two centimeter Luer hypo-

dermic syringe... As this was my last place of call last night,
I thought it might be—ahum—here."

"Is it?"

"No. Damned queer, too, I say. Ahum. It was in the bag
when I went up to see Roger. Yet it was missing when I
opened my bag this morning at the office. Ahum, odd, is
it not?"

I said, "It—ahum—is." He glared at me. "So somebody
stole it?"

"Why'd you see LeBreque last night?" Hanley interrupted.

"Mr. LeBreque was an invalid. Couldn't walk. Been
bedridden—ahum—for the last two years. Hellish thing.
Marked atrophy of both legs. I visited him every day.
Ahum."

"That's swell," Hanley said. "Goetel could've bumped
him off because he wouldn't let Alison marry him. Alison
could have killed her uncle for the same reason. And as for
the rest of you—Rina, Agatha LeBreque, Walter LeBreque, Dr. McKay, and you, too, Boyle—any one of you might
have kicked him in for a slice of his will. He left enough
mazuma to float a battleship."

Agatha LeBreque got to her feet, snapped, "You're a
fool like all police," and stalked out of the room. She went
upstairs, her cane rapping all the way.

The telephone in the hall rang. I went out and picked up
the handset and said, "Hello?"

"All right, herpetologist," the Old Man began. "Here's
the lowdown on your snake venoms. How's the murder
coming?"

"It isn't coming. It's going. What've you got?"

"Mamba venom affects the vasomotor system in the medulla oblongata. It causes suffocation by paralyzing the respiratory center. Gaboon viper venom is both neurotoxic and haemotoxic. That is, it does what mamba venom does and besides, it destroys corpuscles and makes a man bleed badly. Is that enough?"

"Plenty," I said. "Hang up in a hurry." He did. I immediately called Centre Street and asked for the M.E.'s office.

"I'm on the *situs criminis*," I said, when I got Dr. Kyne, "and thirsting for erudition. Was the venom which killed Roger LeBreque hemotoxic or neurotoxic?"

"Both," said Dr. Kyne. "I'll give Hanley the actual content after the post mortem Monday. Now don't bother me. I'm busy." He hung up.

I went back to the living room and had just arrived there when the telephone rang again. Hanley answered it, and this time it was for him. When he came back, triumph had pervaded him. He exclaimed:

"Babcock checked that handprint! It belongs to Tony Ragna, a small-time crook with a record that reads like a timetable! And what's more, Babcock picked him up not five minutes ago and slapped him in the can!"

"On what charge?"

"Grand larceny. And he's talked!" Hanley whirled around and pointed his finger at Walter LeBreque. "Did you hear that, mister? Tony Ragna's talked. And you're the guy who hired him to burgle your brother's room! Get your hat, LeBreque. You're coming down to headquarters with me right now!"

LeBREQUE DIDN'T OBJECT at all. He sighed tiredly, and

got up. He looked as though he had expected to be found out all along.

I said to Hanley, "Wait a sec, Poppa. Arresting Ragna is ducky. But did he have the green mamba with him?"

"Are you kidding?"

"Far be it from me," I said, "to kid about a green mamba!"

"No, he didn't have it."

"Thanks," I said. "I just wanted to know."

I waved good-by to Hanley and I went out. Sampson was waiting for me on 77th Street. He was talking with the flatfoot, who gaped when he saw me. I gave the cop the bird and told Sampson, "Stick around. Nothing new now. If anything breaks, let me know. I'll either be home or at the Hideaway... Oh, yeah, you might phone the paper and tell them that Tony Ragna has been arrested in the LeBreque case and Walter LeBreque is being detained at h.q. as a material witness. How are you at dodging mambas, Sampy, my boy?"

"Just about willy-nilly," he said.

"Better start practicing," I said casually. "Unless I'm slipping, there's a nice venomous one on the loose somewhere in this house. That's why I'm leaving. So long!"

4

THE VENOMOUS HYPO

THE HIDEAWAY CLUB on Broadway between 42nd and 43rd was as deserted as Death Valley in summer. Latham was in his office when I arrived, around ten-thirty. "What's new?" he said.

"Oh, murder," I said. "Nice fashionable murder."

He blinked. "You on the LeBreque thing?"

"Yeah," I said. "How you come to hear about it already? It wasn't in the morning papers, was it?"

He nodded to the Philco on his desk. "Caught a flash on the air a few minutes ago. So Daffy Dill is going up in the world. Communing with dead millionaires now! That guy's daughter used to visit the Hideaway once in awhile. You know. Rina LeBreque. And I'm here to say she's one cold tomato!"

"Yeah," I said. "She sure knows the answers. She's the kind of a dame who'd tear wings off flies."

"She was a popular kid, though," said Latham, lighting a cigar. He leaned back in his chair. "She used to come here with a different guy at least three times a week. And could she hold her likker! Then she came with one guy steadily for two weeks, maybe. After that, she didn't come at all."

"When did she stop coming?"

"Oh, a month or two ago. Just stopped like that." He snapped his fingers. "It was kind of funny, 'cause she liked her Broadway."

"It would sound," I said, "as though she might've acquired a ball-and-chain."

"Naw," said Latham. "There wasn't a word about her getting married in the papers."

"Exactly," I said, thinking fast. "But there are such things as secret elopements. Suppose the old boy had been against the marriage. Honestly, Bill, he seemed to have had a complex against marriages. Suppose he was. Suppose Rina got married and kept it still so's she wouldn't be disinherited? And suppose the hubby got impatient waiting for Roger to cash in his checks and decided to bump him off instead, so that Rina would come into her millions?"

"You sound like a cop," Latham grinned.

"My God!" I groaned. "Still, the idea's hot, Bill. Only—which one of those mugs would she have married?"

"She couldn't marry Walter LeBreque. He was her uncle. Maybe—I wonder—"

"Who?" Latham asked.

"William Goetel," I said. "Damn, but that would be a honey! That would explain why she hates the other girl, Alison. Alison in love with Goetel and not knowing he was married to Rina. Mammy mine, what a situation!"

"She used to come here with Freddy Brackenworth, sometimes," said Latham. "The playboy of the Fifties. How about him?"

"N.G.," I said. "He's worth plenty. Why would he bump someone for mazuma? She has to be married to a poor guy or it doesn't work. Goetel or Boyle. Boyle! There's a guy!

She might have married Boyle, her old man's secretary! But Goetel would make a better story."

Latham picked up the telephone, chuckling: "Daffy, all you do is think of a story… Hello?… Yeah, right here… It's for you. Sounds like Hanley."

I took the handset. "Hello, Poppa. Merry father's day to you!"

"Cut it out," Hanley said. "Sampson told me you might be at the Hideaway, so I called. It's about that phone call you got this morning. Alison says she did it. But if she was trying to protect William Goetel, then she must have known that murder had been committed, right?"

"Right," I said.

"Well, she said she knew, all right, but how could she? When we got there, the door was locked on the inside. It was a snap-lock. How could she have gotten in? She admits she didn't have a key and she won't tell me who told her."

"Aw, what of it?" I said. "She just doesn't want to get anyone in Dutch with you. Probably Boyle told her. Being the secretary, he must have a key to that door. Did LeBreque tell you why he hired Tony Ragna to burgle that room?"

"Yeah."

"Why?"

"Roger LeBreque had I.O.U.s of his amounting to a hundred grand. He thought if he could get them and destroy them, the debt would *pfft!*"

"Sounds logical. Going to hold him?"

"I've got enough trouble," Hanley said. "Halloran's on my neck. I guess we'll let it drop. It was a family affair anyhow. But it'll hurt my pride to let Tony Ragna back into society."

"Don't turn him loose yet," I said. "Ragna, I mean. I think we might have a nice talk with him on what startled him into leaving a beautiful handprint on that desk."

"Yeah," Hanley said. "Suppose we do that? Meet me at h.q. in about an hour."

"Yea, verily," I said. I hung up. "You know, Bill," I said, "that idea of Rina being married appeals to me. Where would a society dame elope?"

Latham shrugged. "Greenwich, Connecticut, I guess."

"Yeah?" I said. "Dinah and I once tried that. You have to wait five days. When they were up, she'd lost her nerve. Now she wouldn't even say 'maybe' to me."

"How about Westchester, then?"

"Swell!" I said.

I CALLED THE *Chronicle* and got the Old Man. "Never mind the sweet amenities," I told him. "Here's another problem for that brontosaurus brain of yours."

"That sounds," remarked the Old Man, "like a dirty crack."

"The brontosaurus," I said, "weighed twenty tons, four pounds of which were used for thinking. You catch on? Well, listen. I have a hunch that Rina LeBreque eloped some time during the last two months. I want you to check on every town in Westchester County and see if you can find any dope. And if those fail, try Elkton down in Maryland. Got it?"

"Call again some time," the Old Man sighed.

"They didn't find the snake yet, did they?" Latham asked.

I shivered. "No, and that's what I don't like. Snakes are unhealthy things when they're on the loose. And a green mamba—fastest snake in the world. Well—" I got up—"I think I'll mosey on downtown and get a load of Hanley questioning Tony Ragna. I haven't had a good laugh today."

"Remember me to him," Latham said. "So long, Daffy. Drop in again when you can't stay so long."

Tony Ragna was in Bill Hanley's office at the homicide bureau when I got there. He was a thin ginzo and small. Like most small-timers, his eyes were furtive.

"Hello, Poppa," I said, grabbing a chair by the desk. Hanley was grinning at me like a Siamese cat. I said, "Why the grim elation, Adonis? Did Halloran break a leg or something?"

"Daffy," said Hanley, sounding all bubbly like champagne, "the case is over."

"You're kidding."

"Like hell I am! Have a seat and I'll tell you how I did it."

I ogled. "How *you* did it? Why, you chiseling numskull, you never solved even a crossword puzzle!"

"Sore loser," Hanley mocked. "Can't take it when a guy beats you out, eh? Listen to this: I began to figure about that crack you made when you said a snake had two fangs, see? So after Walter LeBreque told me about hiring Ragna here to lift the I.O.U. notes and I saw that the lead was a dud, I poked around upstairs and went through every one's room on the sly."

"What were you looking for," I asked, "a cigar store coupon?"

"I was looking for the hypodermic needle," snapped Hanley. "The one that Dr. McKay lost. Don't you get it, you cluck? Not only was a green mamba missing from Professor Goetel's snake joint, but a tube of viper venom was also gone. So I figured that the killer stole the snake as a blind and really took the tube of venom for the killing. Then the guy took McKay's hypo needle, see? And he filled it with venom and jabbed LeBreque over the heart with the needle."

I was marveling because Hanley had hit the nail on the head. This had been my own theory all along, but I never expected a nitwit like Poppa to ever find it out. I gasped, "Go on, genius!"

"THAT'S ALL THERE was to it," Hanley said. "I found the needle in the bureau in John Boyle's room and I put him under arrest."

"Umm," I said.

"Listen, Daffy," Hanley said. "He's the only one could have done it. There was the needle in his drawer. He had a key to the room. He was in the house all last night. He was there when Dr. McKay was there so he could have lifted the hypo while McKay was upstairs."

"Nice going," I said. "I mean it, Bill. Looks like you've got something. But have you found the mamba yet?"

"No."

"Have you found the tube with the rest of the venom yet?"

"No."

"Have you found William Goetel yet?"

"No."

"That's bad," I said. "And what was Boyle's motive in rubbing out the old gent?"

"Don't know that yet. He won't talk. He says he's been framed, that someone planted the needle in his room." Hanley suddenly looked serious and leaned toward me. "Think maybe someone did?"

"Why, Poppa," I said, "you just told me the case was solved!"

"It is!" He slammed the desk. "Only—there are sorta a couple of loose ends—"

"Hey," Tony Ragna growled.

"When do I git to go home?"

"Shut your trap," Hanley said.

I nodded toward Ragna. "How about this gink? Did he talk?"

Hanley sighed. "He doesn't know a thing."

"Is that a fact?" I said to Ragna. "And why did you leave the print on the desk? Just getting careless in your old age?"

"Say," Ragna leered, "I guess yuh'd've left a print too if you'd lamped the stiff in bed. Baby, that stiff was a birdie! It caught me under de heart and I grabs for de desk. Then I took a powder fast as I could."

"You didn't actually see the murder committed? That didn't frighten you into grabbing the desk?"

"Say," Ragna exclaimed. "If I'd run into that, I'da fainted dead away. I ain't much on bumpin', mister. I don' like it none." He looked at Hanley. "When do I go home, Lootenant? Yuh said yuh wasn't gonna hold me."

Hanley flicked his thumb at the door. "Right now. And keep out of my way, Tony. The Baumes will get you if you don't watch out."

"Oh, I'm gonna go straight now," Ragna lied. "Don' worry about that, Lootenant. I'm goin' straight." He sneaked out of the door as fast as he could.

"Well, Daffy?" Hanley said.

"Pretty well, thanks," I said. "Mind if I use the phone

to call the Old Man and tell him the police have arrested
the murderer of Roger LeBreque?"

"You think I'm right, then?"

"Ah, Poppa, I didn't say that. I said—"

The telephone on his desk cut me off. He picked it up
and answered it. His homely face began to droop like his
big nose. When he finished and hung up, I could see that
News with a capital N had just transpired and that Hanley
and his theories had been blown to hell.

"Stop looking like a surprised wife!" I snapped. "What's
happened anyhow?"

His jaw moved, but no words came out. He gulped,
spluttered, finally took the dead cigar from between his
teeth and gasped, "Agatha LeBreque's just been killed!"

The hair on my neck rose. *"What?"*

"Murdered! The same way as her brother! All bloody and
swollen and discolored! Snake poison! But how? I got the
hypo needle right here! And if she was just murdered—
then how could Boyle have—"

"You've been taken, and at your age!" I got to my feet.
"All right, master-mind! Let's get out there before somebody steals your watch!"

5

DOUBLE-CROSS

AGATHA LeBREQUE WAS dead, all right. There were no two ways about that. Her face looked pretty awful. The venom seemed to have centralized there and it did ghastly things. Another phase that wasn't so pretty was that eye of hers. The evil one. The other was shut tight. The evil eye was wide open, shining like glass, staring sightlessly....

And the iris had not dilated.

We didn't waste any time. Doc Kyne got out there, but couldn't tell much without an autopsy. He had the wagon take the body to the morgue and then we went to work.

Claghorn, who had been left behind in the LeBreque house until things were cleared up, said, "The old dame got tired after you took Boyle down to headquarters. She said she was going up to take a nap. That girl"—he pointed at Alison LeBreque—"went with her and came right down."

Hanley groaned. "But where was everybody? I haven't been gone more than an hour! Didn't you check? Which one of these people could have gone up and killed her?"

Claghorn shook his head. "Not a one of 'em, chief. Walter LeBreque was right here. Rina was right here. Alison was right here. They were in this room all the time!"

Hanley gaped. "But—but—ye Gods!"

I said, "Listen, Claghorn, who found the old girl dead?"

"I did," he said. "I thought I heard someone calling for help. I went up. She'd just passed out when I got there. She was still warm and her nose was still—"

"Never mind that," I said, seeing Alison just about ready to collapse. I turned to Hanley, "Poppa, these three couldn't have done it. Boyle, in the calaboose, couldn't have done it. That leaves two people."

"William Goetel and Dr. McKay!" Hanley breathed.

"Right!" I tore into the hall, after I got the medico's number from Rina, and I called his office. A nurse answered and gave me McKay immediately. "Where've you been for the last hour?"

"Right here, ahum! Right here in my office! What is the meaning—ahum—of this latest outrage? I've been attending my patients. My regular office hours! Ahum, my senator shall certainly hear of this—"

I hung up. "He's got an alibi," I said.

"Give me that phone!" Hanley yelled. "Spring 3-100... Hello? Homicide bureau and make it snappy... Hello, Halloran? Listen, Inspector, this is Hanley. I'm out at LeBreque's again. Have you heard—oh, you have? Well, get this: The man we want is William Goetel. Put it on the wire. Pick him up... Hell, chief, he's the only one who *could* have done it! And listen, get John Boyle out of the can before he starts thinking of a suit for false arrest! I'll see you at h.q."

He slammed down the receiver and brought out a new stogie to chew on. Anyway," he said gruffly, "we know where we're going now."

"I know," I sighed, "where I'm going. Home. The seren-

ity of my humble abode appeals to me at this moment. And
I still cannot say in truth, that this resplendent mansion is
a haven of safety...."

"Meaning what?" asked Hanley dourly.

"Meaning," I replied gently, "that no mention of the
finding of that vicious and venomous green mamba has
reached my eager ears. And until such tidings do emanate
out of the blue, I prefer remaining in localities as far
removed from this sector as possible. If there are any
more corpses, save them until Monday. We don't put out
a Sunday edition."

WHEN I GOT back to my apartment, the telephone was
ringing to beat the band. I closed the door and went over
and picked up the hand-set, Saying, "Your nickel. Give."

"Well, it's about time!" said the Old Man with grim
satisfaction. "We checked Westchester for you on that
Rina LeBreque marriage hunch you had. You were hot.
She's married, all right. She was married on April 12th in
Portchester!"

"To whom?" I asked quickly.

"John Boyle."

I heaved a long, sad sigh.

"What's the matter? The hunch dead?"

"Chief," I said, "half an hour ago, that news would've
gladdened this old heart of mine no end. Hanley arrested
Boyle and had him in the jug without a motive. His being
married to Rina gives him plenty of motive—the LeBreque millions—or part of them, at least."

"Well, isn't the idea still good?"

"It's terrible," I said. "While John Boyle was in the jug,

someone bumped off old Agatha LeBreque in exactly the same manner as Roger kicked in."

"Holy Harry!" the Old Man yelled. "Why didn't you phone, you four-flushing imitation of a pencil-pusher? Don't you know we're running a newspaper here? Or do you? Who did it?"

"Only one guy could have done it," I said. "William Goetel. And he's on the wire now. They're spreading out a dragnet. They'll get him before tonight. And now stop yelping and give me Brad for rewrite. What more do you want on my day off?"

It didn't take Brad long to get the yarn down. When he had it, I hung up. My doorbell rang at exactly the same time. I went over wearily and opened it up. And I found myself looking straight into the black barrel of a gleaming nickel .32 caliber revolver, over which there hung a terrified young face and a pair of desperate gray eyes.

"Please, please my weak heart," I said nonchalantly. But I didn't feel nonchalant. I didn't like the nervousness of his trigger finger and the muzzle of the gun was too close.

"I'm—coming in," he said, blurting.

"By all means," I said. "But would you mind removing your aim from my left ventricle? I'm fond of that one."

He came in and slammed the door. I tried to be casual. I took out a cigarette, lighted it, and sat down. He looked at me for a long time without saying a word. He was quivering like a leaf. The gun weaved in his hand. His face was pasty with pure terror and his lips bloodless. He looked like a nice kid, for all of that.

I said, "Well?"

"I'm William Goetel!"

"Yeah," I remarked dryly. I eyed the revolver. "I sort of got that idea!"

"Listen, Mr. Dill," he said sharply, "you've got to help me. They're hunting for me all over the city! And I didn't do it! I swear I didn't do it! I wasn't near there when Agatha LeBreque died! I only heard it in a coffee shop over on Madison Avenue! It came over the air! You've got to help me!"

"I could help much better," I said, "without worrying about that gun in your hand. It's bad for my health."

He twisted the gun down and shoved it in his pocket. "I'm sorry," he blurted. "I didn't mean to scare you. There aren't any bullets in it. And the hammer's broken. I just carried it for bluff, in case you tried to phone the police about me. Gee, Mr. Dill, I've been trying to see you all day long, ever since Alison told me that she'd call you and get you to help me out. I didn't kill old Roger. My God, I couldn't do that! You've got to believe me and help me."

The kid was sincere and honest. You could tell it in his eyes. "Sonny boy," I said, "you get me. But there isn't much I can do now." I shrugged. "If you didn't do it, then an outsider did. The rest of that crew have cast-iron alibis. Where have you been all day? Suppose you park the carcass and relate."

He nodded nervously and sat down. "Around a quarter of eight this morning, Alison telephoned me at Dad's place and told me that Roger was dead, murdered. She thought someone was trying to frame his murder onto me, so she told me to hide while she got in touch with you. That's about all. But I didn't do it. Gee, Mr. Dill, if I ever wanted to murder anyone, I wouldn't have done it with venom. That would brand either my Dad or me right off."

"That father of yours," I said, "is so absentminded he'd set out to kill someone and forget who it was by the time he got under way."

He smiled wanly and nodded.

"I don't see what can be done," I said. "None of those other people could possibly have killed Agatha."

"Mr. Dill—you've got to believe I'm innocent!"

I nodded soberly. "I do, kid. Take it easy. I'm afraid you'll have to face the music. If I could think of anything—"

"ISN'T THERE ANY possibility," he asked, "that Agatha could have been killed without the killer being on the scene?"

"I don't think—" I started to say automatically. Then I stopped and stared at him. "By damn! You've got something there! Sit tight!" I turned and grabbed the telephone and called police headquarters. They gave me the M.E.'s office right away, Doc Kerr Kyne answering.

"Vulture," I rattled, "this is Daffy Dill again. And get this. It's important. The whole case hangs on it. Have you looked over Agatha LeBreque's body at all?"

"Yes," Dr. Kyne answered nasally. "Although it's none of your business. And don't call me 'Vulture!'"

"All right, Buzzard. Don't quibble. How was that venom administered to her?"

"Don't know," he snapped. "Not a mark of injection anywhere on her body. I just called Hanley about it. Damn queer, I say."

"Not a mark?" I cried. *"Are you sure?"*

"Sure I'm sure," he replied. "Guess I know my business.

Not a mark on her body where either fangs or hypo needle could have made an injection." He paused. "I suppose *you'll* tell me how it was done?"

"You bet your sweet life I will!" I shouted. "Her eye! Her left eye! It's a phony, Buzzard! It's glass, a counterfeit. You take out that eye and then tell me what you find!" I gulped for breath. "And phone back here. My apartment. I'm waiting. Make it fast!" I hung up.

Goetel stared at me. "What do you mean by that, Mr. Dill?"

I grinned. I felt pretty good. "If he finds what I think he'll find, all your worries are over, friend."

Goetel looked puzzled.

We waited around ten minutes. The suspense was killing. And then the phone rang again like the "welcome home" sign on a doormat. I grabbed the handset. Doc Kyne said, "Daffy?"

"Yes, Buzzard?"

"I've got to hand it to you. And don't call me 'Buzzard'! You guessed it that time. That's how the venom reached her."

"Why didn't it hit her while she was erect?"

"The hole was up too high. She had to be prone for the venom to flow. Anything else?"

"I could kiss you, scavenger! Yea, verily! Where's Poppa?"

"Hanley's in his office."

"Listen, doc, switch this call over to his bureau, will you? And thankee, neighbor, thankee for a scoopy that is a scoopy! And don't give it out until I break it in the *Chronicle!* After all, it was my idea!"

"All right," Dr. Kyne grumbled. "All right. I'm switching the call. Wait a minute...."

Goetel tugged at my arm. "What's happened?"

"Something that can clear you!" I said. "Here's how Agatha LeBreque was murdered: The killer of Roger knew Agatha had a glass eye, see? Glass eyes are hollow. And usually, people take them out at night for the sake of cleanliness, get it? So the killer took the glass eye—or substituted another one—and bored a tiny hole through the glass in the upper part. The venom of the Gaboon viper was then poured in and the hole was sealed with cocoa butter or something else which would melt at body temperature.

"The moment Agatha laid down, after she had that eye back in her head, the venom would flow through the aperture into her optical cavity, where there would be plenty of open space for entry into her system. But she had to *lie down* to make the venom flow. When she was standing, the level of the venom inside the glass eye was *below* the hole. As soon as she was prone, the hole in the eye was on the bottom and the venom could drip through!"

"But that means—"

"Sure," I said. "It means she was carrying a poisoned eye in her head all day long from the moment she got up that morning. It remained for the killer to get as far away from the scene as possible and wait for her to lie down, get murdered, and thus give the killer a perfect alibi, being away when the deed was supposedly done!"

"Mr. Dill!" Goetel exclaimed, less nervously. "You sound like you know who did it!"

"My friend," I said, "I will bet you my entire salary for the year to come that the man who killed Roger and

Agatha LeBreque was none other than—" I didn't get a chance to finish.

Hanley broke in on the wire while Goetel gasped.

"Yeah, Daffy?"

"Listen, Poppa. Things are moving. This time, we let the killer walk right into us. Are you with me? Don't answer. You are. Now get this. Do you know where Tony Ragna lives?"

"Yeah. Little place on 14th Street. Small apartment. Number 136 East. Why?"

"You beat it over there as quickly as possible. Tony is going to blackmail the killer and the killer is going over to Tony's to silence him and you and I will be there when the event comes off."

"Are you nuts?" Hanley roared. "Tony Ragna can't blackmail the killer! He doesn't know who did it! It was the corpse he saw, not the actual murder and murderer!"

"Sure, sure," I said. "You know that. I know that. Why? Tony Ragna told us. But he didn't tell the killer!"

"Smart," Hanley said. "What's the gag?"

"I'm phoning a guy," I said. "I'm going to be Tony Ragna. I'm going to blackmail like Tony. I'm going to make an appointment at 136 East 14th Street immediately. If the guy is guilty, he'll be there. If he isn't, he won't show up. It's a double-cross, Poppa. A sweet double-cross, and the killer is on the short end for once in his life!"

6

COBRAS AND MAMBAS

TONY RAGNA'S APARTMENT was a dirty little two-room place that hadn't been cleaned since it was built. Tony was scared to death. He thought there would be gunplay, and he didn't like the idea of being the bait.

There was a battered alarm clock on a decrepit mantel. It had a tick reminiscent of a couple of sledge hammers hitting rock. It seemed to make the seconds years. We stood there, Hanley hidden in a closet directly opposite the door, his service .38 in his sweaty hand, myself directly behind the door with a bent poker in my right fist, Tony in a chair, sunken down, haggard, terrified.

I'd been there ten minutes. Hanley twenty. And still no sign.

Five more minutes passed.

It couldn't go on. Ragna was cracking already. Sweat dripped from his face. I had my wind up. It was hard to breath easily.

And then the steps sounded out in the hall. They were cautious steps; slow, sure, but the planking in the hall was old, and a creaking gave each step away. They came to the other side of the door and there they stopped.

I held my breath.

Three solemn and distinct knocks rapped out on the door. I frowned at Tony Ragna and nodded at him savagely to answer.

Ragna clawed at his throat and sat up straighter. Hoarsely, and with an effort, he croaked, "Come in."

The door opened slowly. Into the room stepped John Boyle.

"H-hello," Ragna faltered.

"Hello," Boyle said, his tones steely. He stepped in farther and closed the door firmly. By doing that, he exposed me to sight. But he kept facing Ragna. He didn't turn. He didn't see me. "Are you the rat who called me?"

Ragna went white.

"You wanted to be paid off, didn't you?" Boyle said evenly. "You wanted to be paid off in a lump sum, didn't you?" Ragna just stared at him. Boyle's hand went down into his pocket. It came out with a small pistol in it. A little thing with a pearl handle. A .25 caliber toy. But a toy that could kill. He cradled it, leveled it at Ragna. "Well, rat, I'm making one payment. But I'm making it in lead, not gold."

I clipped, "All right, Boyle! Drop the rod! You're covered!"

Which all went to show how much I had underestimated the little secretary's make-up.

He whirled around instantly and fired twice before I could even move an eye. The bullets didn't miss me, but they didn't hit me, either. They made a twin set of holes on the left side of my coat, slapping against the old plaster wall.

I let the poker ride the ozone. It caught him across the right cheek, opening a nasty gash and sending him down to the floor, where he dropped his gun.

With the blood pouring out of the gash, he grabbed the pistol and went up on his right knee, aiming it squarely at my stomach.

I yelped, "Hanley—don't kill him!"

Boyle's lips went up in a sneer. "That's an old one, you dirty—"

Simultaneously, Poppa Hanley's revolver went off with a roar like a young cannon. A black hole appeared on Boyle's gun hand, while the toy pistol flew across the room.

I'll never forget the look of intense surprise on Boyle's face as he stared at the bullet hole right through his palm. Then I stepped over before he could move and clipped him cleanly on the point of his thin chin.

The door burst open as he fell over. William Goetel ran in, yelling, "Are you all right, Mr. Dill? Are you all right?"

I said, "I told you to stay downstairs."

Hanley stepped out of the closet. "And who is that monkey?"

"William Goetel," I said. "Nice shooting, Poppa."

"You're a cluck," said Hanley. "Some day you'll know better than to play hero and jump a gun."

"Yeah," I said ruefully. "Lookit that coat. Do you know a good tailor where they can match materials?"

AFTER WE GOT back to Centre Street with the quarry I called the *Chronicle* while Hanley put him in the jug, and I gave Brad the whole yarn from top to bottom and side to side.

I had just finished spieling when Poppa came back from the cell block looking a ghost without a house to haunt. He wailed, "Daffy, something is very phony!"

"What now?" I said wearily.

"The green mamba!" he said. "We can't find that damn snake!"

"What?" I said. "Didn't Boyle—"

"Hell, he talked all right! He said he got the test tube of Gaboon viper venom from Professor Goetel's serpentarium two days ago. He was in the place with the professor and he sneaked the tube out. He just took one at random; he knew they were all poisonous. The professor never knew the difference. Boyle counted on the gink's absentmindedness. Well, he kept the venom and after the blowoff last night between young Goetel here"—he motioned toward Will Goetel who was still with me, having tagged along— "Boyle figured the time had come for action. He was sick of waiting around for the old man to die. So when Dr. McKay came, Boyle went downstairs and lifted the syringe. Last night he filled it with venom, stole in there and gave it to Roger over the heart."

"That checks. Go on."

"He hid the syringe in his own drawer because he wanted himself to be arrested. That was part of his plot. But meanwhile, Agatha was asleep and had taken her glass eye out. He bored that hole in it and filled it up with the rest of the venom. Then with some cocoa butter, he closed it. That was his alibi. While we had him nicely arrested, he counted on her dying and thus freeing him."

I said:

"And she darn near did! Thank the Lord for Tony Ragna as a wedge for blackmail. But what about the mamba?"

Hanley groaned. "Boyle says he didn't steal the snake and he doesn't know where it is! He was just as scared as the rest of us! He says he wouldn't have handled a green mamba for a million bucks!"

"Green mamba?" William Goetel murmured. "What is this, Daffy?"

I shivered. "You ought to know. Your old man called the cops this morning and said one of his green mambas had escaped. After the murder, we thought the killer had stolen it, but apparently the snake really made a getaway all by itself."

Goetel frowned. "Are you certain?"

"Of course I am! I saw your old man myself. He showed me the den where it had been. There were only three mambas in it. The fourth was missing."

Goetel gasped, stared, then began to laugh uproariously. "Oh, lord! Oh, that's good! That's funny! It's all a mistake, gentlemen, it's all a mistake!"

"I don't get you," I said.

"Why," Goetel laughed, "you yourself said how absent-minded my dad is! That's it! The same thing with his snakes! Walter LeBreque brought him back four cobras and three mambas from Africa. And Dad keeps thinking that he was brought *five* cobras and *four* mambas!"

"What?"

"Sure, only last week he wanted to call the police and report that one of his cobras was missing! He thought he had five instead of four! I dissuaded him in time and saved the taxpayers some money!"

"Well, I'll be double-damned," Hanley whispered.

I sighed with relief. "Anyway, I told him he was Public Enemy Number One with his memory. Boy, I'm going to get a kick telling this choice parcel to the Old Man. It'll make him rave!"

And it did.

I COVER CRIME

Daffy Dill Follows a Tangled Trail of
Theft and Murder That Begins with the
Corpse That Tried to Smoke Cigarettes

1

THE CORPSE ON BOARD

IT WAS SUNDAY, twelve noon, when I reached the *Chronicle* building down on West Street. No sooner had I got inside the swinging doors than Solly Hanson—who writes all the ship news for the paper—grabbed me by the arm and tore out shreds of his own hair.

He chattered: "For Pete's sake, Daffy, where in hell have you been? Sampson has been trying to get hold of you for the last hour. He's been calling here every five minutes on the dot!"

"Such energy," I said sitting down on Solly's desk. "What'd he want?"

"Something about a murder. I didn't get it all, he talked too fast."

"A murder on Sunday?"

"That's what he said."

"But that's impossible," I said. "I have a theory about that. Nobody murders on Sunday. Six days shalt thou work and the seventh vacation. You know... Did he leave any address?"

"Naw," Solly grunted, "but he'll phone again any minute. Get off my desk. You're sitting on tomorrow's colyum."

I got up and simultaneously Solly's phone jingled, so I

*Hanley shot the beam
of the flashlight
into the hole*

picked up the handset and said: "This is Daffy, Sampson. What is it?"

"Gee whiz," Sampson said breathlessly. "Where've you been? It's a murder! A honey, too! You'd better get down here and cover. It's out of my territory."

"Where are you?"

"Forty-Second Street ferry," he said. "I've been calling you every time the tug docks."

"You mean—the corpse is on the ferry?"

"I'll say it is!"

"Who's in charge, Inspector Halloran?"

"No. Bill Hanley. He wants to see you."

"I'll be right over," I said and hung up.

I caught a taxi down on West Street. We rode hard up the viaduct, there being neither traffic nor cops along the way and we made the ferry slip in something like seven minutes flat.

When the ferry finally docked, I walked down to the end of the pedestrian lane to see if I could find Sampson on board. There wasn't a sign of him. Then I heard someone calling: "Daffy! Oh, Daffy Dill!" I looked up. There he was on the boat deck, waving his arms frantically. "This is it! Get on and come up here!"

I boarded the tub and went f'rw'rd—as the tars of the briny say—and finally reached the first lifeboat on the port side. I think it was the port side. I never can figure out which is which. There was quite a crowd. The official police photographer had his camera up and was shooting beautific studies of the cadaver. I saw the Buzzard—Dr. Kyne to you—the department's chief medical examiner who gets sore as a boil when I call him the nickname. Two of Halloran's second grade men, Claghorn and Babcock, were there.

And, of course, Lieutenant Bill Hanley, who helped make the homicide squad as notoriously efficient as it is, was in charge. He said soberly: "Hello, Daffy. Glad to see you."

"Hello, Poppa," I said. "The same to you."

His homely face was screwing back and forth as he chewed his unlighted cigar. He called to the photographer: "You finished, Louie?… Okay, take those plates right down and develop them. How about it, doc? What's the dope on this?"

DR. KYNE SNIFFED stuffily. "The dope," he said with dignity, "is simply this: He was killed not more than nine hours ago. Strangled to death as you see. No other signs of violence. No blows, contusions, abrasions or lacerations. Just strangulation. That's all."

I said dryly: "And apparently enough, eh, Buzzard?"

He ignored me and handed a slip of paper to Hanley. "Here's your removal order, Lieutenant. I'll have the post mortem in your office tomorrow morning. Good day, gentlemen, and Mr. Dill."

He strutted off and disappeared down the staircase. "The funny part is," I said, "he can't get off the boat until we get all the way back to New York."

Hanley shrugged. "He's just sore. Had to come all the way in from Westchester. He was playing golf… I suppose Sampson told you?"

"Sampson told me nothing."

"Then have a look here… Babcock, pull back the tarpaulin and give Daffy a squint at the stiff."

There was a man lying in the bottom of the boat. He was half sitting, his back resting against one of the crossbeams, his legs sprawled in opposite directions across the hull. He was medium-sized, about fifty-five or sixty years old, gray-haired, wizened face, with a thick nose and gray eyes. The eyes were wide open, popping almost. So was the mouth, with the tongue protruding. Hanging from the left side of his mouth, still attached to the lip, was an unlighted cigarette. It was gold-tipped, and on the side of the white paper were the initials *V.P.*, as plain as the nose on Hanley's face.

He was dressed in a somber topcoat, an Oxford gray suit which was too sedate, and beside him in the bottom of the boat was a black derby, its band uninitialed.

Around his throat was twined a piece of cord. It was smoothly waxed and very thin. It must have been as sharp as a knife. I could only see it under the ears. On the throat itself it was hidden between the rolls of flesh which its pressure made.

"Nice job," I said distastefully. "Who is he?"

Hanley shook his head. "We don't know. No mark of identification at all, except the initials on his cigarette. We had a deckhand up here who was on the night shift last night and he said this guy came on board around four o'clock, acting sort of nervous. That's all."

"And not too much," I said. "Tell you what we'll do, Poppa. I'll have Sampson take one of the photos down to the Old Man and we'll run it tomorrow under a caption: WHO IS THIS MAN?"

"Okay," Hanley said. "I'll have Claghorn check the Bureau of Missing Persons."

Claghorn grunted. "That never works."

I glanced at my wrist watch. It said quarter of two. I told Sampson: "You write this yarn, demon. Give it a couple of sticks. It's not important until we know who he is."

"Gee, Daffy. Think of the novelty. Ferry boat, Punjab noose and all—"

"Names make the news," I said. "When we get a name for him, we'll have a story. Until then, he's just another corpse on the barroom floor. Take a photo down with you from h.q."

"Don't you kind of think he's a man about town, Daffy, with the monogrammed cigarette and all?" Hanley asked.

"Sure," I said, "if the cigarette is his. I wouldn't bet on it, though. He's dressed like a butler. For all you know, he may live in Jersey City. Otherwise, what was he doing on a Jersey-bound ferry-boat at four a.m.?"

"Good thought," Hanley said. "I'll check over there too."

The ferry had docked on the Jersey side. By the time I got down on the main deck, the autos were all starting up and trying to get off. I looked around for Dr. Kyne and found him standing on the river-side of the ferry and regarding the murky river morosely.

I said plaintively: "Listen, Doc, all kidding aside. I'd like to know something."

"Well?" he said coldly.

"Was he strangled from in front or in back?"

"From the front," the Buzzard said.

"Then he saw the man who killed him?"

"Quite likely."

"Did the expression on his face give you the impression that he was surprised at the act?"

Dr. Kyne nodded. "You want to establish the fact that he not only saw his murderer but also recognized him? I should say that was exactly what happened."

"Then the look of surprise means that he was killed by someone he thought was a friend."

"Quite possible."

I sighed. "I'm sure glad the killer wasn't his enemy. We might have had to brush up the pieces and paste them together in order to have a *corpus delicti*. Thanks, anyway, Buzzard. See you around the Tower of Silence."

"Not if I," Dr. Kyne replied acidly, "see you first!"

2

THE ILLEGITIMATE JEWEL

AT A QUARTER of three, I stopped off in a drug store on the corner of Madison Avenue and Fiftieth Street and pulled out a telephone book.

I had a date at three with the wealthy and flighty Mrs. Jane Powell, a popular widow of the Fifth Avenue set, but in making the engagement, Mrs. Powell had neglected to give me her address and I had equally neglected to ask her for it at the time.

I couldn't find her name under the P's, nor could I find Valerie Powell, either, who was her charming and beautiful daughter and whose photo never missed a week in the rotogravures of the Sunday papers. But I did find a Van Powell who had a Fifth Avenue address near Seventy-Second Street. I parted company with a perfectly sound nickel and called his number.

I was right. It was Mrs. Powell's house, so I took a cab up to Seventy-Second and Fifth. It was exactly three when I got there. The place was a three-story sandstone house, wedged in between two resplendent apartment houses. It looked sadly cramped. It had a basement like the old speakeasies on Fifty-Second Street and a flight of stone steps to the front door.

I went up them and rang the bell. Valerie Powell herself opened up for me, smiling sweetly. She looked pretty as hell in a lavender summer suit and she seemed to reflect the rich color of her plum blouse.

I grinned at her. "What—no butler?"

She laughed pleasantly. "Hello, Mr. Dill, do come in.... As a matter of fact, our butler is absent without leave. It's really scandalous but he didn't come in at all last night."

She took me through the hall to the living room, which was furnished in good taste, despite the idea I had that Mrs. Powell went in for the frilly things. There was a man there. He was dark-haired, pasty-skinned, around thirty years old. Valerie said: "Mr. Dill—Mr. Meredith. Now both of you sit down. Smoke?"

"Thanks," I said. "Say, is Van Powell your brother?"

"Yes."

"I didn't know where you lived. Tried to find it in the phone book. That was the only Powell that looked like the mark."

"I know," she replied. "Mother has a private number."

Meredith didn't say anything. He looked politely interested in the conversation but he plainly wasn't listening. Presently, Mrs. Powell came downstairs and he instantly came to life, springing up expectantly as she entered.

Mrs. Powell was ebullient. "Good afternoon, Mr. Dill! So nice of you to come!..." Then to Meredith: "Danny, be a good boy and run along now. I have business with Mr. Dill. *Private* business, you know! Valerie—show Danny out.... My, isn't it warm today!"

She sat down in Meredith's vacated chair while Valerie took Meredith out. He was openly disappointed. When he had disappeared, Mrs. Powell said: "Danny's such a dear boy, and he'll make an exceptional lawyer. He has such an aptitude for lying!" She giggled. I joined her politely. Valerie came back and said: "All right, mother. He's gone."

"Oh? Oh, yes… Now what was it—"

"The emerald," Valerie said patiently, smiling at me.

"Oh, yes, the *emerald!*… Mr. Dill, you come to me very highly recommended as a young man of resourceful daring and skill."

I said: "Recommended by whom?"

"Why, Wilston Kenyon, of course! He's quite proud of you!"

Wilston Kenyon III is publisher and sole owner of the New York *Chronicle.* I reminded myself to hit the Old Man up for a raise and to give Kenyon as a reference. Would that burn him!

"Now about the emerald," Mrs. Powell said. "I must tell you now, Mr. Dill, that word must not get out. You see, Mr. Dill, when I was in Cannes last winter, I treated myself to the most exquisite emerald! I couldn't possibly tell you how lovely it—"

Valerie interrupted: "You digress too much, mother. I'll tell him. Mother bought this stone abroad last winter. When she returned to this country, she attempted—for some inexplicable reason—to smuggle it in without paying the customs tax on it."

"Just a girlish whim," Mrs. Powell beamed. "It was such a thrilling adventure!"

"WHAT'S MORE," VALERIE went on, "she succeeded in getting it through. She gave it to Mr. Meredith and he carried it in concealed in the top of his derby."

I said: "What was the stone worth?"

"Seventy-five thousand dollars," Valerie said calmly.

I whistled. "You shouldn't have smuggled that one. If they ever find out, they'll slap a fine on you that'll break your heart"

"Oh?" Mrs. Powell said, looking wistful.

I said: "Well, what's the trouble?"

"The stone has been stolen," Valerie said.

"Yes," Mrs. Powell added, "and the theft puts me in a dilemma. I can't report it to the police because I didn't declare it at the customs. It—it isn't insured for the same reason."

I sighed. "And I suppose you want me to get it back for you?"

"That's it exactly. I'll pay you five thousand dollars when you do!"

"Five grand?" I exclaimed. "Lady, you just hired me... When did the emerald disappear?"

"Three weeks ago," said Mrs. Powell. "I'd worn it to a reception and when I came home, I put it in my jewel box on my dressing table. Ordinarily I put the jewel box in my wall safe, but that night I forgot to. Next morning, the emerald was gone. I didn't know what to do about it. Finally I asked Mr. Kenyon for a man I could trust. He recommended you."

"Three weeks ago," I muttered. "That's bad. It might be cut by now. You say you bought it in Cannes six months ago?"

She nodded. "At Knight Brothers, Limited."

"And the first time you left it out of the wall safe, it was stolen? Who was with you that night?"

"Danny Meredith. Just we two." She smiled. "And he left before I took the stone off. It's a pendant, you know."

"And where were you?" I asked Valerie.

"In Louisville at the Kentucky Derby," she smiled. "I went down with Mr. Conrad Myers."

"No chaperon?"

"Mrs. Powell tittered. "They're just about engaged to be married, you know, Mr. Dill."

Valerie stiffened. "Don't be silly, mother."

I took stock. Dr. Conrad Myers was a society doctor with plenty of mazuma. When he performed an appendectomy, he got front page publicity because his clients had names that made news.

Finally I said: "And your butler?"

"Herman Kroll," Mrs. Powell said. "He was here, of course."

"Any maid?"

"None."

"How about your son—Van Powell?"

She flushed and looked uneasy. Valerie stepped to her side and said: "Van was away, Mr. Dill. And I'm sure I don't see what connection he could possibly have with mother's stone disappearing."

I shrugged. "I was just asking…" I got up. "I'll look into it, Mrs. Powell. I've got to push off now. I'll give you a ring when I learn anything," She nodded, smiling, and Valerie showed me out.

I walked over to Madison Avenue and found another telephone booth. I dropped in a nickel and called the *Chronicle*.

Sampson answered. "Hello, Daffy? Nothing new on

the ferry killing. Hanley is going to check on the clothes tomorrow. He found a label in the topcoat."

I said: "Sampy, my boy, you're going to save Poppa a lot of bother. Get this: The name of your corpse is Herman Kroll. He's a butler in the employ of Mrs. Jane Powell of Fifth Avenue, who resides in a redoubtable edifice which is a hangover from the ancient regime, the number being 1165."

"Holy socks!" Sampson cried "How'd you find that out?"

"It's the bloodhound in me. The story is all yours. Keep my good name out of it, understand? You tell Poppa Hanley I tipped you off, but I want no implication in the thing officially, at all. You catch on?"

"Allee same catch," he said. "But whose cigarette was it? If his initials are *H.K.*, then whose are *V.P.*?"

"That's for the homicide squad to figure out," I said. "Keep your own nose clean and ask the Old Man for a by-line on that yarn. You're coming up in the world."

3

THE MISSING MAN

ON MONDAY MORNING, about a quarter of nine, just as I was busily superintending the boiling of a dropped egg, the door opened and Bill Hanley walked in.

"Hello," he grinned, pulling up a chair at the kitchen table. "Just coffee for me."

"You're welcome," I said laconically. "Sometime you must stay for dinner. I see you got your man."

He raised his eyebrows. "Herman Kroll, you mean?"

"No," I said. "The guy who killed him."

"How can you tell?" he marveled.

I shrugged. "The gleam in your eye. Why else would you be here at this hour of the dawn. Go on. Tell me. And pour the coffee yourself. I'm late for the office."

"Daffy," Hanley said, "I want to know something. How did you know that stiff was Kroll?"

"The Powells were missing a butler. That added to the fact that I was offered and smoked a cigarette in the place which was gold-tipped and marked with the initials *V.P.* sold me on the idea."

"And you were dead right," Hanley nodded. "It was Kroll all right. Want to know who bumped him?"

"Dying to hear, Poppa." I started on my egg.

"Van Powell."

I took a sip of coffee and didn't say anything for a few seconds. Finally I asked: "What gives you that idea?"

"I'll tell you. When Sampson tipped me off, I took a photo of the stiff and went up to the Powell place. When the old lady identified the picture and heard the bad news, she did a pass-out. My God—what a dippy dame she is! When she came to, she yelled for her medico."

"Dr. Myers?"

Hanley nodded. "He came over, but that was later. I worked on her, figuring the shock would give me an advantage. It did. She opened like an umbrella. Listen: Kroll had been working for her less than a year. Apparently, he had no friends, no enemies. He seldom went out, preferring to remain at the house in his room. Okay—Saturday night, when Dr. Myers brought Valerie Powell and her mother home from Latham's Hideaway Club where they'd been for the evening, Kroll was at the house, alive and well. That was at three a.m., really Sunday morning. At four a.m., one hour later, he was strangled on the ferry and dumped in the lifeboat."

"Did you check alibis?"

"I'm getting to that. Mrs. Powell and Valerie were home in bed, so they say. Dr. Myers was home in bed, so he says. Dan Meredith was home in bed, so he says."

"What about that Meredith?"

"A nobody. Small job, clerking for a law firm. No practice of his own yet. He's on the make for Mrs. Powell."

I laughed shortly. "For her money, you mean." I finished eating and got up. "Anyone else?"

Hanley nodded. "There was a guy named Hogan," he

said. "Bart Hogan. But I couldn't locate him at all. Eight years ago, he and Kroll were convicted of a petty larceny charge. They were in stir together a year. I thought Hogan might have had something against Kroll in the past, but there's been no sign of him in this burg since he finished his term."

"So that leaves—"

"Van Powell. Get this, Daffy. Three weeks ago, he came home and had a blowoff with his mother. She was sore because he was losing too much money gambling at Jimmy LaVerne's Town Club. Whereupon, he threw Meredith in her face and she told him to get out and stay out."

I asked: "Where did he go then?"

Hanley threw out his hands. "I dunno. He was in a tux. He didn't pack a bag. His mother says he was flat broke—didn't have a dime. He just stomped out and she hasn't seen or heard from him since."

"Isn't she worried?"

"A little. But she says it's happened before, only he's had money other times. When it gave out, he always came back and apologized—until the next time. She said this was the longest he'd ever been away."

I shook my head. "Poppa, you're a gem. I see your idea. Van Powell needed the cash so he telephoned Kroll to meet him on the ferry where he robbed the butler and then strangled him. That's marvelous."

"Never mind the acid," Hanley said. "Maybe the motive is weak, but Van Powell is still the best bet. How did Kroll get one of the kid's cigarettes in his mouth?"

I looked surprised. "Then the V.P. did stand for Van Powell?"

"Sure. Who'd you think?"

"Possibly Valerie. Their names both begin with V.... As for that, Kroll, working in the house, could easily have snitched a couple of Van Powell's cigarettes. They're right in the house. I had one myself."

"Okay, but Kroll didn't smoke."

"What?"

"You heard me. Kroll didn't smoke. Mrs. Powell told me."

I gasped. "But don't you see then—never mind, never mind! Poppa, I never believed you could be so thick. Do me a favor. Can I use the reports of your men?"

"For what?"

"Private biz."

"Tailing reports?"

I nodded. "On Dan Meredith, Mrs. Powell, Valerie Powell, Dr. Myers, and anyone else in the case."

"I've got a man on each of them," Hanley said. "Call me at h.q. now and then and I'll give you the low-down."

"Thanks," I said. "I'll see you in jail."

We parted in front of my apartment house where I boarded a cab and drove downtown to the *Chronicle* building.

4

A DOG AND AN ALIBI

THERE WAS A note in my typewriter. I picked it up. The contents of the note were as follows:

> You oversleeping hound of hell, come in and see me about earning a living.
>
> MAX.

I threw it in the waste basket and went into the Old Man's doghouse, where Maxie was keeping house for the day.

He looked up at me when I closed the door and he grinned. "Did you get the note?"

"I did."

"Hope you appreciated the thing. I wanted to make you feel at home. That's the kind the Old Man usually slips you, isn't it?"

"Sort of," I said, "although I must confess that he sometimes comments tersely upon the illegitimacy of my ancestry. What's on your mind, Maxie?"

"I've got a story for you.... Oh, it's small. But all your big yarns started from little acorns. It came over the AP wire this morning. A howling dog in New Rochelle. The canine has been singing steadily for a week, mostly at night. Get the idea?"

I sighed. "Hiho, Maxie, to think you covet such ghoulish thoughts in that cranium."

Max grinned. "Why not? Howling dog. Maybe a grave. Maybe a corpse. Hot stuff. Maybe murder. Why did the dog howl? Dogs are funny that way about death."

"And indigestion," I said. "Mostly indigestion."

"Listen," Max said. "Today I'm the boss. You cover."

I went back to my desk in the city room and called Kit Roller on the New Rochelle *Standard-Star*. Kit knows Westchester like a book and is one of the best newspapermen in the game.

"Kit," I said, "this is Daffy Dill, more or less troubled about a blatant canine who resides in your vicinity and has been disturbing the peace of your fair city. Can you give?"

"Hello, Daffy," he said. "The dog? What dog?"

"The howling dog of New Rochelle," I said.

"Oh, that! It's nothing at all. A black police dog just raising Cain in the back yard of a house on the Shore Drive. A couple of citizens complained, so I took a run over with the chief of police. A Myrtle Banning keeps house there. The place belongs to a fella named George Anderson. He wasn't around. She said he's away and that the dog misses him and that's why the howling. You ought to hear the poor hound! He can hit high C. He just sits by a flower bed and let's go in a coloratura soprano that a prima donna would give her heart to own…. What's new?"

I said: "Nothing, my friend, is ever new. Remember that and you'll never be surprised. Thanks for a bum yarn."

"Don't mention it," he said. "Call again."

No sooner had he hung up than my telephone rang again. I answered it and Dinah said, "Hoity-toity, Mr. Dill. Valerie Powell of Fifth Avenue and Southampton wishes to converse with you, although I can't imagine why. Are you blackmailing her or something?"

"Cut it out, angel-eyes," I said. "Put her on."

Presently, Valerie said: "It's I. Are you busy?"

"Never."

"Can you meet me for lunch? I've something important to tell you."

"It'll have to be Dutch. I'm flatter than a postage stamp. Where and when?"

"Immediately, if you can make it. I'm at the Tick Tock Tea Room on 34th Street."

"Be right up," I said. "Stand by."

I reached the place inside of twenty minutes.

"Of course," Valerie Powell began anxiously," you've heard about Kroll—our butler?"

"I've heard."

"The police were at our house all day yesterday. I'm afraid mother talked too much. Have you heard anything about—my brother? Van, I mean—"

I LOOKED DOWN at my assorted cold meats and potato salad, which same constituted my lunch, and I murmured:

"He's in trouble. The police think he killed Kroll."

"But he couldn't have!" she cried. "That's why I wanted to see you! Van couldn't have done that!"

"Why not?"

"Because he wasn't in New York when Kroll died! He isn't in New York now!"

I sat up. "You know where he is?"

"Y-yes. He's—in Miami now."

I said: "You've got to give, lady. Van left your house in a huff, three weeks ago, in the middle of the night. He was wearing a tux, he took no luggage and he had no mazuma. Will you tell me how he got to Miami without clothes or money?"

She looked frightened. "I don't know."

"You didn't give him money?"

"N-no! Perhaps he borrowed some from Dan Meredith or Dr. Myers and made them promise not to tell. But Van's in Miami. He's been writing to me!"

"For money? Is he broke?"

"N-no, not for money. He said he was having a fine time and had won a lot of money on the horses at Hialeah Park."

I rubbed my chin. "That's rather supernatural, since the racing season at Hialeah closed on March 28th last. May I see the letter?"

"I—I destroyed it so that mother wouldn't see it. Van asked me not to let her know where he was."

I shrugged. "Okay. Then let me give you some advice. You wire Van and tell him to head for New York right away. If he was in Miami, he hasn't a thing to worry about. But he'd better prove he's innocent before the newspapers make the most of it."

Valerie looked non-plussed. "But, D-Daffy, I—can't do that. He—didn't give me his address. He just wrote to me from Miami."

"That's nice. When did you last hear from him?"

"This morning. The letter was mailed Saturday. Air mail," she added defensively.

I pushed my plate away. "You're lying. You're trying to

cover him up. You're thinking things and you're afraid I'm thinking them too, because you know damn well that the night Van disappeared, your mother's emerald pendant disappeared too! You're afraid I'll find out he stole the thing!"

Valerie stared at me for a long time without saying a word. Her face went white with anger, and her pretty eyes narrowed malevolently. The silence was thick after the barrage of words. I didn't like it.

Finally, she pushed her chair out and got slowly to her feet.

She said very quietly, "You're a fool." And she turned and left without another sound.

So the lunch didn't turn out to be a Dutch treat after all. She left her check behind her and I had to shell out for the both of us. When I had paid off, there were thirty lonesome pennies in my jeans.

5

HANLEY GETS A LETTER

ON TUESDAY MORNING just after I finished scraping and hacking a beard off my tender chin, a telegram arrived for me. I signed for it, tipped the boy and then opened it. It read:

> SORRY TO DISAPPOINT YOU BUT AM RETURN-
> ING EMERALD TO MOTHER MYSELF STOP VAN
> POWELL.

"And there," I murmured, "goes five grand out the window."

The wire had been sent from the Grand Central Station at 9:05. I had received it ten minutes later.

I put on my hat and coat and picked up a little tin badge which I had once bought in a pawnshop. It looked like the real thing and it had the words *FEDERAL AGENT* inscribed on it. You know, a kid's badge. Only when a man sported it, a good bluff could put the thing across.

I went over to Grand Central and found the telegraph office. There was an elderly woman behind the counter, gray-haired and owl-like. I handed her the wire I had received and I flashed my badge just long enough to let her see the words on it.

"The man who sent this is wanted by the police for murder. Did he leave an address here?" I said.

She shook her head. "No doubt, but I can't give it to you. It's against company regulations. I'm afraid you'll have to get permission from someone higher up in order to inspect the files."

"Okay," I lied. "I'll do that. Meanwhile, how about some sort of description. Were you here when he sent it?"

"Yes," she said. "He sent it about twenty minutes ago. He was short and rather stout, I thought. He had on a greenish kind of suit and there was a big ring on his pinky with a red stone. I remember because I admired it."

I nodded. "How about his face? What did he look like?"

"Well," she said, frowning, "he was smoking a cigar. His face was fat and he had thick lips. Oh, yes, he wore glasses. They had black rims."

"Thanks," I said, and I left.

I got a directory and looked up the address of Dr. Conrad Myers, the society medico, and Mrs. Powell's port in a storm when her exophthalmic goiter made her eyes pop. He had an office on Fifth Avenue and 43rd Street, not two blocks from where I was.

When I got there, I had to wait in his reception room while he gave some nice-looking young lady's tonsils a going-over. The nurse was young and capably good-looking. She talked to me while I sat there.

Finally the young lady made an exit. I rose and went into Dr. Meyers' private office, where I found him seated at a desk. His layout was resplendent, the kind a country bumpkin dreams about all his life. Myers was a big man, around six feet tall, black-haired, thin-faced, his clear blue eyes set closely together. His mouth was small, his lips narrow. He said, "Yes, sir?"

"My name's Dill," I said. "Daffy Dill. You may have heard of me."

Myers nodded, somewhat coldly. "Valerie Powell told me about you and your mission for Mrs. Powell."

I smiled. "Did she tell you anything else?"

"I don't understand."

"About her brother, perhaps, being wanted for murder?"

He looked down at some papers on his desk. "I'm afraid that is none of your business."

I snapped: "I'm afraid it is, Dr. Myers! Where is Van Powell? Valerie says he's in Miami. This morning, I get a wire from him in New York. Or was it from him? Is he short and fat? Does he wear glasses and smoke cigars?"

"Of course he doesn't," Dr. Myers replied warily.

"All right. Then he didn't send the wire. Is he in Miami? Did he write to Valerie from there?"

Dr. Myers bit his lip. "So she says."

"I'm asking you, doctor. Do *you* know? Van Powell was dead broke and wearing a tux when he stepped into the mist three weeks ago. Where did he get money and clothes to get to Miami?"

"I'm sure," Myers replied, "I don't know."

"Yes, you do," I said. "You gave it to him. Why don't you admit it? You can help him out of a jam if you admit it. If he's in Miami, then he's innocent. If he isn't, you'll be hit for obstructing justice. You can't stand to have your reputation hurt."

HE DEBATED THIS a long time. Finally he said, "I'll play ball with you, Dill. I did give Van money to get away. He came to me that night and told me what had happened. He asked for a loan. I gave it to him. Then he left. He said he was going South."

"How much did you give him?"

"A thousand dollars."

"Can you prove that?"

"I don't see how—"Myers stopped suddenly and brightened, "But of course, the canceled check!" He got up and opened a private file. He took out a bank statement, searched through a pack of canceled checks and finally found the right one.

It was dated three weeks before and made out to Van Powell for the sum of a grand. I turned it over. He had endorsed it on the back. Right under his name was another endorsement, that of a George Anderson, with the notation: *For deposit in the Corn Exchange Bank & Trust Company.*

"Who's George Anderson?"

"How do I know?" Dr. Myers said. "I gave it to Powell. He must have given it to Anderson when he cashed it."

"That's something, anyhow," I said. "I'll keep this, doc. I've got to check the endorsement."

He said: "By all means!"

"Thanks," I said. "See you around." I left the office and went back to the reception room, where I grinned at the nurse, then stared at Dan Meredith who was sitting there, nursing his left hand. He said coolly, "Hello. You too?"

"Not me," I said. "What happened to you?"

"I caught my hand in a door," Meredith said reluctantly.

"It looks okay to me," I remarked.

"Well, it isn't!"

I frowned as I left. No reason for him to get so sore. I went downstairs, and called Poppa Hanley.

"Listen, sleuth," I said, "this morning I got a—"

"Hold everything!" Hanley exclaimed. "Listen to what I've got to unload! We located Kroll's bank account. Savings. He had five thousand dollars in it, deposited two weeks ago! Where did he get a lump sum like that? You don't know? Okay! Then listen to this. This morning in my mail, I got a nice little ditty from—guess who?"

I said: "Van Powell."

"Right! And guess what it said?"

"My hunch," I said, "is that it was a confession having to do with the murder of Herman Kroll."

Hanley gasped. "Say—how in hell did you find it out?"

"I just guessed," I said. "Was it typewritten and signed?"

"Yeah… What are you, a spiritualist?"

"And now I suppose Van Powell is on every teletype and every shortwave broadcast in the country?"

"You're damn right he is, and none of your sarcasm, Daffy. I may be thick, but when a guy sends a note, says, 'I killed Herman Kroll,' and signs his bona fide signature, identified and sworn to by his sister and mother, I've got a case!"

"Where and when was the letter mailed?"

"Last night at ten-thirty in Grand Central."

"All right," I said. "I'll show you why Van Powell didn't kill Herman Kroll. It won't hurt your case any because the D.A. will be able to laugh at this. But you may see the light. Get this: *Kroll did not smoke.* You told me that yourself. Then Kroll, naturally, did not take one of Van Powell's monogrammed cigarettes on his own. You assume that Van gave him the cigarette. The hell he did. In the first place, Van Powell would have known that Kroll did not smoke. In the second place, Kroll would have refused any proffered cigarette because of the fact that he did not smoke."

Hanley sounded quizzical. "What are you getting at, Daffy? The point is good."

"This is what I'm getting at," I said. "That *V.P.* cigarette was stuck on Kroll's lip after he had been strangled. What does that show? Kroll knew the man who killed him. The Buzzard told me that. But the man who killed him didn't know Kroll well enough to be aware of the fact that Kroll did not smoke. And there's your killer!"

"Fine," Hanley grunted. "And who is it?"

I said sadly: "That's the one catch. I don't know yet." And I hung up with a sigh.

6

TWICE ILLEGITIMATE

WHEN I GOT to the office, Dinah told me that Maxie Trotter was all in a dither and wanted to see me right away. Outside of that, Mrs. Jane Powell had been trying to get in touch with me and asked that I call her immediately upon arriving.

I did that little thing right off.

"Oh, *Mr.* Dill," she said in an excited, high-pitched voice, "I'm so sorry to have put you to any trouble on my account, but I am afraid that I must withdraw my offer of five thousand dollars for the return of my emerald. It's *back*, you see, safe and sound!"

"When did it arrive?" I asked.

"This morning in the post. My son had taken it… Van, you know. Just a boyish prank. I've quite forgiven him."

"How do you know he took it?"

"Why," she said, "he mailed it to me last night and he had a return address on it."

"What was the return address?"

"Why—" She thought a second. "Oh, yes—4413 Sheridan Square. Valerie tells me that it's down in Greenwich Village somewhere. Valerie's gone down to see Van. I do hope he'll get over his foolish pride and come home like a good boy."

I said: "I'm afraid Valerie won't persuade him, Mrs. Powell."

"Oh? But why not?"

"Because Van won't be there."

"Won't be there?"

"No," I said. "He won't be there, for the simple reason that there is no such number as 4413 Sheridan Square."

"Oh!" she cried, and I hung up.

I went into the Old Man's doghouse where Maxie Trotter was and I asked:

"Okay, guider of destiny—what's the daily rub?"

Maxie exclaimed: "It's that dog again—that damn howling dog! He's news this morning!"

"News?" I grinned. "What happened? Did a guy bite him?"

"Don't be a cluck," Max said. "He's been shot. He'd been yelling so much, they put a bullet into him. Phone New Rochelle and get the details."

"Yea, verily," I sighed and exited to my desk where—in the turbid gloom of my cranny—I called Kit Roller on the *Standard-Star.*

"Don't tell me, don't tell me," he said buoyantly. "It's about the dog, the good old howling dog of New Rochelle. Right?"

"Right," I said. "I hear that some one has bumped off the poor beastie in first-class style. Bullets and everything."

"That's right. He died like a dog," Kit said.

I groaned: "Forego the puns and give, brother, give."

"Well," Kit said, "it was this way. Yesterday afternoon,

George Anderson, the man who owned the pooch, telephoned police headquarters and told them that his dog was
beyond any obeying commands. Anderson couldn't shut
the hound up and the baying was getting on his nerves.
So h.q. sent a patrolman over. There was a lot of ceremony.
Anderson really liked the dog, it seemed, but the ole howl
got him down. I was there and saw it. The dog just sat by
that circular flower bed where the nasturtiums grow and
yodeled obstreperously. Well, the patrolman, a nice guy
named Gunning who hated to do it, finally put a bullet
through the dog's skull. Then Anderson took the body over
to the S.P.C.A. place for disposal."

"Listen," I said, "this guy, George Anderson. Tell me
something, Kit. What does he look like?"

"Oh," Kit said offhand, "short, fat, wears glasses, always
smoking a cigar. And the most nervous cuss you ever did
see."

"What's his racket?"

"He's a got small jewelry store on Elm Street. Makes
phony stuff and sells it to shopgirls. He also sells real stuff
when people will buy it, which is seldom—from the dimin-
utive size of the store."

I said: "You're a big help. Thanks, Kit."

No sooner had I hung up than I lammed out of the
offices and took a cab uptown to a pawnshop on Madison
Avenue which was run by a nice old fellow named Harold
Rosecrans. I told him that I needed him for about half an
hour and that it would be worth ten bucks to him to come
along, so he joined me in a cab.

We rode up Fifth Avenue to Mrs. Powell's house. My
name went over and we were admitted to the living room

where Valerie immediately harnessed me with: "Daffy—what's happened to Van? Where is he?"

I didn't know and I told her so. Before she could ask any more questions, I cornered her mother and asked to see the returned emerald.

Mrs. Powell was flustered. "But really, Mr. Dill—why?"

"You'll see," I said. "Maybe I'm wrong. Maybe I'm right. If I'm wrong, you'll pardon me. But let this man—Mr. Rosecrans, Mrs. Powell—see the stone, please."

She nodded. "Valerie, get my emerald, please."

VALERIE WENT UP and came downstairs again. She had the pendant in her hand with the glowing green emerald hanging over the edge of her hand. She avoided my eyes and gave it to Rosecrans, who took a small magnifier from his pocket, slipped it under the flesh of his brow, and examined the stone.

He gasped in a moment. "But-good God—this is not real!"

Mrs. Powell cried sharply: "What are you saying?"

"Not real!" Rosecrans exclaimed. "This is paste, an imitation."

I said: "That's all I wanted to know. Come on, Harry.... And Mrs. Powell—I presume that your offer still holds good for the return of the emerald—the real emerald?"

She nodded dumbly. She was still nodding when I pulled Rosecrans out into a taxi behind me and rode downtown as fast as I could taunt the driver into driving....

Leaving Rosecrans in front of his store and a sawbuck richer, I went west to my apartment where I telephoned Bill Hanley. I asked: "Anything new on your end?"

"No," he said. "Just what I told you."

I said: "Any sign of Bart Hogan—the man who was in stir with Kroll eight years ago?"

"I think he's dead," Hanley said. "We haven't been able to trace him at all. He went West—California we think—but he disappeared after he reached there. Nobody ever heard of him again."

"All right," I said. "Give me your report on yesterday's activities of Dr. Conrad Myers and Dan Meredith."

He gave them to me. They were the dullest reports I ever heard, but when he was reading the tail-end of Myers', one little item caught my attention and held it.

"—Dr. Myers then went to the Grenada Hotel grill for dinner where he met another man who joined him. Stranger was short, fat, wore glasses, smoked cigar—"

"That's enough," I said. "Now, listen, Poppa, I think I've got a great big surprise for you. If you'll be a good boy until I can get some more evidence to cinch the thing, I'll tell you tomorrow."

"Sure," Hanley said sourly. "Maybe you'd like a game of tiddley-winks with me sometime." He hung up.

No sooner had I done so than my telephone rang stridently and I hastily retrieved the handset and said: "Hello?"

"Daffy Dill?" A man's voice, low, muffled, hoarse with excitement.

I said: "The one and only."

"Listen," he said in desperation, "I've got to see you! I'm in a jam! You're the only one who can help me! Valerie told me—"

I said: "Whoa, brother. The name, please?"

He hesitated momentarily, then: "Van Powell."

"Where are you?" I clipped.

"I'm—I'm phoning from the Times Building. Can you come at once? It's urgent!"

"I'll come," I said. "You get on the shoe-shine stand in the basement and stay there till I get there. Right?"

"Right," he said, "only hurry."

I hung up and went to my desk and took out the .32 pistol which I own. I slipped it into my pocket. Then I went out and down the stairs. All the way, I kept thinking about Van Powell, the phony wire, the phony address on the package his mother had received. And I thought about how the emerald had been illegal once—in getting into the country—and was illegal again, because it was a phony. Twice phony. That was an all-time record.

When I reached the vestibule downstairs, I pulled out a cigarette and started out. I thought better of it, because there was a slight wind which blew out my match, so I stepped back inside in order to get a light without any trouble. That saved my life.

No sooner had I got inside than a rattle of gunfire broke out from across the street, and the glass windows of the vestibule doors fell like the Roman Empire.

The bullets made whizzing noises as they ricocheted in the vestibule, dangerously close to me.

I pulled out my pistol and lammed from the vestibule, diving down behind the stone battlements on each side of the entrance stairs.

The shots had come from an alley across the street. No sense firing. I couldn't see anyone there. I got up and ran across the street, zigzagging all the way. No more bullets came at me, no more barking shots.

When I reached the alley, it was deserted.

I followed it through and came out on Sixth Avenue. There was a big crowd walking up and down the stem, but nobody in it whom I recognized. It was hopeless.

I stood there in the alley for a long time, thinking hard. Finally I slipped the gun back into my pocket and sighed. I muttered:

"Hell, Poppa. Why wait until tomorrow?"

I stepped out, caught a cab on Sixth Avenue, and told the driver to head for Centre Street.

7

WHY THE DOG HOWLED

NO MOON, NO stars, no street lights, only the thick darkness. We were standing in the back yard of George Anderson's house in New Rochelle on the Shore Drive. There was Hanley, grim and pallid, who held the beam of the flash on the circular flower bed where the orange nasturtiums flowered. There was Claghorn and Babcock, each with a heavy shovel, flinging up the soft brown earth of the bed. There was the Buzzard, Dr. Kerr Kyne, looking silently interested for one of the few times in his life, holding his black Boston bag in his left hand. And me, knowing what we would find—and dreading it.

An hour before, by arrangement, Kit Roller had brought over a detective from New Rochelle headquarters, and taken George Anderson and his housekeeper, Myrtle Banning, over to headquarters to answer a few harmless questions about the dog. That was the only gag I had been able to figure in order to get them away from there and allow us to work without any protest or show of warrant.

The house was black as pitch now. And silent too. Only the scraping, sometimes jarring sound of Claghorn and Babcock's shovels broke the stillness.

They were down two feet and going strong. It was apparent that the flower bed had been dug deeply, not in the dimensions of a grave where ordinarily a body would be buried lying horizontally. This bed was no more than three feet in diameter, a circle, which went straight down. It was not meant to look like a grave, and it didn't.

Five minutes more, and then Claghorn went white, gasping, as he pointed. Hanley shot the beam of the flashlight into the hole. An odor of rotting flesh seeped up through the dirt, a nauseating stench. Claghorn had uncovered a foot covered by a patent leather shoe.

Hanley said: "All right, boys. Careful how you go now. Don't break the bones."

"God," was all Claghorn could grunt.

Ten minutes later, the dirt was off the thing entirely. It had been a man. Now it was a horror. We pulled it out of the hole with ropes caught under the arms. It had been shoved into the hole with its legs sticking up parallel with its torso. It had stiffened in rigor mortis and as we dropped it hastily on the topsoil, the legs stayed up over the head just as they had in the hole. It made me feel sick.

Hanley reluctantly played his beam of light all over the thing. It was clothed in a Tuxedo, the white shirt now a brown mess. The face was rotted, but there was enough of it to recognize that it was one and the same as the photo which I had in my pocket and which I had got from the morgue of the *Chronicle*.

Hanley looked at me, his face ugly from the sight. "Is it—"

I said: "Van Powell, Poppa."

Hanley shuddered and motioned to the Buzzard. Dr. Kyne pressed forward and stooped down, examining the corpse with his eyes only. He said at length, "This man has been dead all of three weeks."

I said. "Poppa, you realize now, of course, that Van Powell did not kill Herman Kroll. Van Powell was dead before Kroll died. Van Powell was dead when you received his confession in the mail."

"But how in hell," Hanley asked, visibly shaken, "did he get a signature like that on paper when he was dead? His own family identified it."

I reached into my pocket and pulled out a canceled check. I handed it to him. "Turn it over. See there—the endorsement? I'll bet you five-fish I could forge that signature with a ten-minute practice so that Van Powell himself would have identified it as his own. He had a simple fist, easy to copy."

He nodded. "Okay. I'm sold. Now what? Did Anderson do it?"

"No," I said.

"Did he know the stiff was in his back yard?"

"He did.… But listen, Poppa. You're not going to arrest him. When he comes back from New Rochelle h.q., you're going to question him very simply, and when he tells you that he knows nothing about it, you're going to believe him and then you're going to leave. From then on, you tail him and don't lose sight of him. And when he reaches the end of the trail, I'll be waiting for you and you'll hear the blowoff."

Hanley shook his head. "I don't like it, Daffy. I don't like things I don't understand."

"You'll understand all right," I said. "Play ball. I'll see you later."

"Where're you going?"

"Back to New York," I said, "where the trail ends."

DR. CONRAD MYERS lived at an apartment-hotel. He had a suite of rooms on the ninth floor of a high-class stall named Chatsworth Terrace, which was located on Central Park South.

I reached there at ten-ten and I went right to the desk and said, "Dr. Myers, please. I'd like to talk with him on the phone before I go up."

The clerk nodded absently. "Just tell the switchboard girl when you call," he said. "You'll find the phones over there."

I went over to the opposite wall and picked up one of the handsets located in small open shelves and I asked the operator to give me Dr. Myers' apartment. She did so. He answered immediately with: "Hello?"

"Good evening, Dr. Myers," I said. "There is a young lady down here who wishes to see you. A Miss Powell."

"Of course," Dr. Myers exclaimed.

"Send her right up!"

"Begging your pardon, sir," I said, "Miss Powell asks you to come down to the lobby."

He said: "What's that? I don't understand. Let me speak to her."

"Yes, sir," I said. "Just a moment." I held the mouth-piece and waited a couple of seconds. "Sorry, sir. She says for you to come down. Most urgent. She says she cannot speak on the phone."

"Very well," Dr. Myers said, puzzled. "I'll be right down."

"That," I replied, after I had hung up, "is all I wanted to know." I tore for the elevators and waited there behind the branches of a potted palm tree. In a few minutes, one of the cages came down and disgorged the doctor and I quickly hopped into it, said, "Ninth floor," and went up.

I found his door number and prayed that the door would be unlocked. It was. I went in, closing it gently behind me, and I stepped into a clothes closet in the little hall next to his living room where I sat down on the floor, my gun in my hand, and waited.

Myers came back in ten minutes, slammed his door angrily, and locked it. I could hear the click. His footsteps disappeared into the living room and the place grew still.

I sat there.

At eleven-fifteen by the radium hands of my watch in the dark of the closet, someone knocked at the door.

Dr. Myers hurriedly answered it. It was Anderson, excited, babbling. He exclaimed: "Doc, my God, doc, they've found him! They found young Powell! Tonight they—"

His words faded as they passed into the living room. I stepped out of the closet and to the door, which I promptly unlocked. That was for Poppa Hanley, so's he wouldn't have to use an axe. This done, I stepped to the edge of the living room, stood behind the portieres and listened.

Myers asked: "When?"

"About an hour ago," said George Anderson. "A dick from h.q. came over and took the housekeeper and me back to ask some questions. It was a steer to get us outa the house. While we were there, the New York cops arrived and dug him out!"

Myers snapped: "How'd they find he was there?"

"I don't know, doc! How in hell do I know? But they've taken the body off for an autopsy. Don'cha see? They'll find out he's full of digitalis and where'll you be? That reporter knows Powell came to you that night because he has the canceled check! That check was swell stuff for proving that Van was alive—as long as he wasn't found—but now that he is, it's a rope around our necks!"

Myers' face was contorted with fury. "It was your damned dog! I'll bet it was that mutt! I'll bet he led Dill to the thing! If I could only have got him this afternoon—"

"Yeah," Anderson breathed. "You shouldn't have missed. What are we gonna do, doc? Take it on the lam?"

Myers got to his feet. "Nothing else to do. Let's get out of here right away."

"But the stone, doc, how about the stone?"

"We'll take it along," Myers snapped. "Damn that dog! This was perfect; it shouldn't have missed! You saw yourself the police thought Van Powell—wait. I'll get the stone."

He went to his desk, unlocked one drawer, then unlocked another drawer inside the first one, and took out a velvet box from it.

Anderson gulped. "I don't like carrying that stone. We should have had it out before this. Hurry up, doc, let's get the hell outa here! I know a place where we can—"

"**FRY IN THE** chair," I said, stepping out and covering them. "It's been nice knowing you boys, very nice indeed.... Hand over the emerald, doc. And so help me, I'll give you a leaden kidney if you try an off-side play."

"*Dill!*" Myers said sharply. Anderson caught his breath, went white. For seconds they were transfixed, did not move. The medico's face went red, then blue, then white, like a dying man who can't get oxygen.

"The emerald," I repeated.

He nodded dumbly and walked toward me slowly. When he reached me, his eyes bored into mine as though they were trying to understand how I was there, how I had broken through the maze he'd constructed. He handed me the velvet box and I took it.

Simultaneously, Anderson—sweating with terror—made a break for the door.

I swung the gun around on him. Myers watched the barrel leave the line with his belly. It was the break he had hoped for. He reached forward, grabbing my gun wrist with his left hand, the pressure forcing the muzzle to the floor.

And with his right hand, as I tried ineffectually to jab at him, he landed a haymaker on my jaw with force that lifted me off the floor and completely out for several seconds.

The gun went off when I hit, and Anderson screamed. I couldn't see anything. There was a black curtain inside my eyes, covering my retina. I couldn't feel anything; I was numb. But I held onto my rod with a grip that couldn't be broken. They would have had to cut off my hand to get that gun.

Instinctively, when I could think again, I swayed to my feet and started for the door. I felt drunk, I staggered like a toper, but I reached the door.

I didn't see Anderson anywhere, although later I found him right at my feet in the hallway with a slug through his thigh. All I could see was the elevator boy, unconscious in the corridor, a welt on his cheek, and Dr. Conrad Myers at the controls of the elevator, glaring at me like a madman, and swiftly starting to drop down from the ninth floor.

I fired at him just once, blindly. I saw the little hole in

the glass doors with its jagged radiating beams. The elevator disappeared, then jerked to an abrupt halt on the floor below.

I found the stairs, careened down them.

When I reached the elevator bank on the third floor, there was the lighted cage stock-still, Dr. Myers on the floor with a gaping hole in the back of his head where my bullet tore away his skull on the way out.

He'd never do an appendectomy again. He was dead.

The controls of the elevator—being automatic—had jerked the cage to a stop when he fell, releasing his grip on the elevating handle.

While I stood there, another cage flashed by the floor, going upstairs. Poppa Hanley was in it, his face set. Wearily, I climbed back upstairs to Myers' suite. When I got there, Hanley was bending down over Anderson and slapping his face.

"Hello, Poppa," I said, sighing.

"You all right, Daffy?"

"All right," I said. "Work on him." I went inside and picked up the velvet box with the emerald and slipped it in my pocket.

Hanley kept slapping Anderson's face and saying, "All right, Anderson, come out of that, come out of that."

"Anderson?" I said, laughing shortly as the man opened his eyes and groaned. "The hell he is! Poppa, you wanted Bart Hogan. Well, you've got him right in your power."

"What?" Hanley cried, jerking the man painfully to his feet. He shook him. "Hogan, you dirty little rat, are you going to talk?"

Anderson, alias Hogan, wilted, his face dripping perspiration. "I'll sing—I'll sing," he groaned, and then collapsed.

SING? HE POSITIVELY shouted. He told the whole story as though he'd written it a thousand times. He didn't omit a thing, and I hadn't either in my own private theory of the mess.

Myers, it turned out, was a regular Jekyll-Hyde baby. He had made a lot of money, playing society doctor, but with the depression, his collections had toppled. He didn't retrench. He was used to money and he wanted money. Holding plenty of Van Powell's I.O.U.s, he approached the boy, put up a proposition whereby Van would lift his mother's emerald in return for his I.O.U.s. Myers argued with the boy that since the stone had been smuggled in, the mater could do nothing about investigating the theft.

Van Powell refused.

Having been thrown in with Hogan, alias Anderson, a small-time jeweler and fence, Myers learned that Kroll had served time with Hogan eight years before. Holding this over Kroll's head as a threat against Kroll's job with the Powells, Myers persuaded Kroll to lift the jewel the first night it was left unguarded.

Kroll did it.

Coincidentally, that same night, Van fought with his mother and stormed out.

What a break for the enemy! Van went to Myers and asked for a loan. He walked right into his own murder. Dr. Myers needed a man to take the theft rap. He also remembered that Van would immediately suspect who had done it when he learned the stone was gone.

Van was given a one-grand check, which he immediately

endorsed and returned to Myers, a thing which should have made him suspicious right off. Meyers then pumped him with enough digitalis to kill a dinosaur. Was Anderson present?

He was. He saw it. Van was then taken to New Rochelle and buried. Anderson then endorsed the check too. Kroll, for his good work, was given five thousand dollars. That was in the savings account Hanley uncovered.

But why had Kroll been killed?

Because, Anderson told us, he had become greedy. Realizing the stone was worth seventy-five thousand dollars, he threatened to squawk unless Myers came across. Myers agreed.

That Saturday night (Sunday morning really) when he brought Mrs. Powell and Valerie home from the Hideaway, he told Kroll to meet him on the ferry. Kroll did and died. Myers planted one of Van's cigarettes in Kroll's mouth, intending to have the police always after a specter. It wasn't a bad idea. It might have worked, if Kroll had smoked.

After Kroll's murder it was only up to Myers to keep establishing the fact, now and then, than Van Powell was alive and on the lam. He had Anderson make a copy of the stone when I got too hot on the trail. The copy was sent to Mrs. Powell, obviously to get me off the case. The telegram was sent by Anderson to impress me with the fact that Van was alive, not dead.

The same with the forged confession Hanley had got.

But when I found out about the check, and when I found out about the phony jewel, Myers got leery. He tried to kill me. Valerie, innocently enough, had informed him that I had found the stone false.

Of course, when Anderson was tried, the stone came in for plenty publicity. Mrs. Powell not only paid a tax, but also a five grand fine. Only her position prevented a jail sentence.

Anderson got the chair. Accessory before and after the fact.

When the whole mess was over, Valerie invited me up to the house one day and handed me the check her mother had promised on the return of the stone.

I wouldn't take it. I said, "I knew she'd get a fine like that. I figured if she got used to the idea of paying out five thousand to get it back, it wouldn't hurt her so much. I don't want it."

I did, however, want to know why she had lied to me about Van being in Miami.

She said: "But Conrad Myers told me that. He was afraid that Van had really absconded with the emerald. I tried to cover Van up, thinking he was hiding out there with mother's stone." She sighed. "And all the time, he was—

"Well," I said, "don't think about that. How do you feel now—about the doctor?"

"I hated him, you know," she said quietly. "Mother wanted me to marry him. I—well, I knew he had Van's I.O.U.s—and I was nice to him. But marriage?" She shuddered. "His eyes—were too close."

"Yeah," I said absently, remembering the little black hole in his head between them. "They were, weren't they?"

TWENTY-THREE MILLION

Daffy Dill Talks with a Dead Woman—
Finds a Murdered Murderer—and Solves
the Mystery of the Hotel Law Suit

1

MURDER IN MANHATTAN

WE HAD BEEN talking about the war and a story in the papers that they were sending twenty-three million dollars in gold to the U.S. because things were so cock-eyed in Europe, and we were saying we'd like a chunk of that ough-day, when Bill Latham remarked: "I see by the papers as how Bomber Malone has busted out of that nice new jail up at Wainsong."

I said, "It's a fact, my friend, it's a fact. He made a crush-out last night and he hasn't been seen since. Bill Hanley was telling me this morning as how the cops have been trying to locate some of the Bomber's mob."

"Well, well," Latham said, grinning, "can't they be found?"

"Uh-uh," I said, "They can't be found anywhere. They've been lying low ever since Bomber Malone went into stir."

Short McGinnis, who throws the giggle-water to and fro for the paying customers of the Hideaway Club which is owned, operated, and inhabited by Latham—a nice guy when you don't owe him money—put my third old-fashioned on the bar in front of me and said, "I heard the Bomber's gang sort of broke up after his conviction."

"Phooey," I said. "They broke up like concrete. They're

hiding, that's all. They've been waiting for Bomber Malone to pull this crush out before they went to work again. Them is the viewpoints of Daffy Dill, comrades, and them is on the level."

I was sitting at the bar in the Hideaway Club guzzling old-fashioneds and trying to forget that Dinah Mason had refused to marry me for the one hundred and ninth time. It was ten o'clock and all was as well as could be expected. Latham felt pretty good. There was a big crowd and the golden coins were filling up his cash register. It'd been a slow day with the *Chronicle*. The war news out of Ethiopia was splashing across the front page, and even the killers of New York had taken a day off to find out all about the hostilities.

I sat there, watching the crowd and keeping an eye peeled for spot news while Latham and McGinnis kept on considering the jail break of Bomber Malone, and then the telephone behind the bar jingled a couple of times and things started in a great big way.

Shorty McGinnis answered the phone and said, "Sure, he's here." And then he turned to me and handed me the handset and whispered in a bass that could be heard in Hoboken across the river, "It's the Old Man, Daffy!"

"So what?" I said. "He can't frighten me. I'm a big boy now."

Shorty grinned and I lifted the handset and said, "Hello, Rasputin. Don't you ever go home and sleep? They'll be calling you the Banshee of Broadway if you don't watch out!"

"That's terrible," the Old Man said sarcastically. "Me— who hasn't set a foot on Broadway in two years."

"All right," he said,
"hand over the letter"

"All right, all right," I said undismayed. "You set your tootsies down every day on West Street, don't you? We'll make it the Wraith of West Street then. What's on your mind—if you have one...."

"Sometimes," the Old Man replied nastily, "you get very irksome. Now see if you can get this the first time. A guy named Jordan telephoned you here and said it was urgent. I told him I'd try to locate you and he said he'd call back in fifteen minutes. Shall I have him get in touch with you there?"

"Nothing doing!" I said. "I'm on my daily nocturnal vacation. Tell him to go jump in the lake. In the first place, nothing could be more urgent than another old-fashioned. In the second place—I don't know any guys named Jordan, I never did know any, and I don't want to know any. In the third place, I'm busy in the first place."

"Listen, Daffy," the Old Man said impatiently.

"Phooey," I said just as impatiently, "from me to you."
And I hung up.

LATHAM CONGRATULATED ME and ordered me another
drink and I was feeling pretty good. Just then, some one
came alongside the bar and said in a low firm voice, "Daffy
Dill?"

"In the flesh," I said and I turned around.

It was a woman. And what a woman! She was around
thirty, dark-haired, with blue eyes as big as marbles and a
skin you'd love to clutch. No kidding, she was a knockout.
She was dressed in a smart brown suit and she wore a crazy
little hat away on the back of her head.

She smiled at me disarmingly and said gently, "My name
is Vivian Merritt."

I got off my bar seat, clicked my heels together and
bowed very low. "Madam," I said, "the pleasure is all
mine...."

"That's it," she said. "Keep joking. I've got to talk to you
alone. It's urgent, a matter of life and death." I stared at
her momentarily. She was smiling prettily. She went on,
"There is a man following me. He means to kill me. Don't
look so serious."

I grinned from ear to ear and said, "Are you on the level?"

"I'll say I am," she replied softly. "Will you help me?"

"I'll say I will," I said blithely. "Who do you want
bumped off?"

"Never mind that," she said. "Just protect yourself, that's
all. I'm going out now. Follow right behind me. Outside,
I'll get into a cab. Get in with me and be careful."

"Let's go," I said. "See you later, Latham."

"So long, Daffy!" Latham called.

Vivian Merritt smiled at me once more, then turned and weeded her way through the crowd until she reached the outer foyer. I kept right on her heels. She turned once to make certain I was following her and then she went into the revolving door and disappeared.

I hopped in the door and when I came out on Broadway, I saw her getting into a yellow cab right under the Hideway Club canopy. I glanced around once, saw a tall thin man with a black mustache in the foyer inside. He was staring at me quizzically. Then I wheeled, skipped across the sidewalk and jumped into the cab beside Vivian Merritt, slamming the door shut behind me.

"Central Park!" she snapped.

The gears clashed and we moved off into the Broadway traffic, heading uptown toward Fifty-Ninth Street.

We both settled back on the leather cushions and she heaved a relieved sigh. "Thanks a million," she said, her voice taut now. "I don't know what I'd have done if you'd refused—"

"Refuse a lady in distress?" I said. "Not on your tintype, madam, not on your tintype. And now, if you will be so kind—"

"I'll explain," she said. "I want information. I think you can give it to me. You cover crime for the *Chronicle,* don't you?"

"In a nice quiet way," I grinned.

"You know something about this man they call Bomber Malone?"

"Sure," I said, eyeing her cannily. "I know as much as anyone else. He was convicted of first-degree murder four months ago but he got away with life instead of the chair. If that's what you mean—"

"No, that isn't it!" Vivian Merritt said crisply. "I know all that, probably better than you do. I want to know this: where is he now?"

"Bomber Malone?" I stared at her.

"Yes. He broke jail last night. Where is he now?"

I laughed and said, "Lady, the police department would give plenty to know that very thing. You flatter me. *I* don't know where he is."

"You don't?" She looked disappointed. "Not at all?"

"Hell, no!" I said. "He could be in the Coco Islands for all I know."

"Damn!" she said.

"Listen," I asked, "what is this? Who are you anyhow?"

Just then, the taxi driver called out of the side of his mouth, "Hey, boss!"

I said, "Yeah, Pegasus?"

"Are you expecting anyone?" he asked gruffly. " 'Cause we're being tailed—whether you are or not. Take a look."

I TOOK A look. There was another cab about half a block behind us, coming along very innocently. I squinted and tried to get a look at who was riding inside, but the other cab was too far back and I couldn't see.

I turned around then and I said to Vivian Merritt. "Listen, mystery woman, this is getting my goat. You said you were being followed by a would-be bumper-offer. Why, who is he, and what's the idea?"

"Dill," she whispered hoarsely. "I'm—" Her voice faded. "Listen—"

I leaned over toward her. "What's the matter with you?"

"—shot—" she gasped.

Her suit coat fell open. She had on a white blouse. Only, it wasn't white any more. It was red with blood, flowing from a hole right in the middle of her chest.

"God," I said. I grabbed her. "How'd—"

"Listen," she faltered. "No—time—explain. Letter—in bag—you take it—give it to Jordan—"

"Who?" I snapped.

"Jordan—" she said faintly. Her breathing was coming hoarse and loud. "Snake-ring on left hand—Jordan—give to him—"

"I'll do it," I said rapidly. "Listen, kid, sit up here and take it easy. Hey driver! Get the hell to a hospital!… Listen, now, give it to me straight. Who got you?"

She sighed, and for a second, I thought she had died. Then her lovely eyes fluttered open and her lips moved. The words barely came out, "Bomber—Malone—stop him—"

As we passed under an arc-light, the glow fell on her face. Her eyes had closed. As I watched, I could see the flesh of her face turn blue, then red, then white, and her breathing, after one last racking convulsive gasp, stopped altogether.

I felt her pulse, could find none at all. Little chills were running up and down my back and I was out of breath, just sitting there watching her.

I grabbed her handbag and snapped it open. The letter was right there, a white envelope all sealed and addressed to *Syl Smith care of General Delivery, Grand Central, New York*. I stuffed it into my pocket, snapped the handbag closed and laid it on the seat.

Vivian Merritt was dead, no mistake about that. Her head lolled on the seat now.

I looked up, saw that we had just crossed Fifty-Ninth Street into the darkness of Central Park. I set my jaw and leaned forward and tapped the driver on the shoulder. I said, "Listen. This isn't the way to any hospital. Turn this jellopy around before I hurt my hands on your skull."

He pulled over to the side of the road and stopped the cab. Then he got to his knees on the front seat and turned around and faced me. I gasped. There was a pistol in his hand, a pistol with silencer over the end of the muzzle.

He said evenly, "What was that, guy?"

There were shadows in the cab and I couldn't see his face at all, but I could see that gun all right.

"All right," he said coldly. "Hand over the letter."

"What letter?" I said.

"Listen," he said in a voice that was colder than an Eskimo's bath, "hand over the letter. I can pick it out of your pocket myself later on. I figure you want to live."

"You figure right," I gulped. I got out the letter and handed it to him. "What is all this anyhow?"

He laughed harshly. "Guy," he said, "you're damn lucky you don't know nothing about it, see? 'Cause if you did, it'd be curtains for you right here and now.... Now get the hell out of here and keep your nose out of other people's business. And if you figure in this thing again, next time you get a pill from Baby here." He patted the gun. "Go on. Lam!"

I opened the door and got out of the cab.

"Another thing," he added as I stood there on the grass by the side of the road. "You tell this to the cops and it'll be curtains."

"I get the point," I said.

He didn't hear me. He had jerked the cab away and even as I stood there, it disappeared around a curve and went uptown through the park.

2

THE MAN NAMED KENNEDY

WHEN I GOT back to Central Park South I headed for a drug store. As soon as I found one, I went in, took up a nice quiet seat in a telephone booth and pulled out the envelope which Vivian Merritt had had in her bag.

Surprised?

Sure, I'd pulled the lamb's wool over the taxi-gunman's glinty orbs. I'd taken him and would he be burnt! He'd asked me for the letter, so I'd given him the letter—which I had received that morning from the telephone company, a dainty little ditty which politely reminded me that I had not paid my telephone bill for two months and went on further to observe that such action was hardly the sporting thing.

Of course, I'd have liked to have given him a letter *without* my name and address prominently emblazoned on the envelope, but it was a quick jam and that had been the only extra letter on me.

I ripped open the letter which I'd gotten from Vivian Merritt's handbag and I wasted no time reading it, feeling at the same time that the name on the envelope, *Syl Smith*, was vaguely familiar. The message ran:

Attack tomorrow, the twelfth, at Eleven A.M. Fergie is

*hopping off for flight at seven A.M. Aurora leaves tonight six
P.M. Finish VM and WJ tonight and we're in the clear. Meet
tomorrow night at the Montauk place nine P.M. Tell Spider."*

And it was signed, *Bomber.*

It was all Greek to Mrs. Dill's little boy, Daffy. It sounded
like the start of some war…*Attack tomorrow.*

I stuffed the letter back into my pocket and then I
started down Broadway, heading for the Hideaway Club
once more. I was just crossing Forty-Eighth Street when
a long black touring car shot around the corner and nearly
severed my connection.

I leaped back onto the curb, figuring for the moment,
that Bomber Malone thought my existence was a pain in
his neck and that he had tried to use the touring car on me,
instead of a bullet. The letter, of course, had been written by
Bomber all right. And there was one sentence which was
pretty clear. *Finish VM and WJ tonight and we're in the clear.*

VM stood for Vivian Merritt… She was finished. WJ
stood for whom? Jordan? The man named Jordan to whom
I was to give the letter, wherever he was?

So I perched on the curbing there like a setting hen and
I crouched back and down in case a gun should start to get
gossipy when who should stick his homely pan out of the
front seat of the car but Lieutenant Bill Hanley, the claim
to fame of Inspector Halloran's Homicide Bureau.

He asked, "Are you laying an egg, Daffy?" and he grinned.

The long black touring car was a police radio patrol
buggy.

"Say," I said lamely, "I'd like to lay an egg—right on
your beezo. Where do you get that stuff—running down
innocent pedestrians?"

"Now, now Daffy," Hanley said drily, "you look very perturbed, you do. Is it indigestion or did you just kill somebody?"

"Kill somebody isn't the half of it!" I said. "I just saw a dame—" And then I stopped, remembering the taxi-driver's last words about curtains if I spilled to the police.

Hanley frowned at me. "What about what dame?"

"Skip it, Adonis," I said. "Where bound?"

"East Forty-Eighth," he replied, nodding his head. I looked into the car and saw his scentless bloodhound, Detective Babcock sitting beside him.

"What's happened?"

"Bump-off," he said laconically. "Some woman. Small fry, I think. Want to come along?"

"While my time is very valuable," I said with supercility, "Life's brightest moments are those when I can insult you, so I shall trip along with you and insult."

"Okeh," Hanley said, "See if you can trip into the back seat without breaking your neck."

I got into the back seat and we were off, cutting across Forty-Eighth Street toward the east side. "We got this call through telegraph bureau about ten minutes ago," Hanley explained. "The janitor of the house went into this apartment to lease some laundry in it, and he found the dame dead. Her name is Green. Cary Green."

"Never heard of her," I said.

WHEN WE GOT there, we found it was a fairly respectable house, three storys, brownstone, and sort of tired-looking. We parked the car and went in and we found the janitor, a frowsy little guy named Furnas, waiting in the vestibule.

Hanley didn't waste any time. We followed Furnas right

upstairs. The corpse lived on the second floor. On the way up the stairs, Hanley got out a cigar and stuck it in his mouth and began to chaw on it unlighted.

The janitor unlocked the door finally, and we went in.

It was a nice little spot, furnished well, clean, sort of cozy. The corpse was lying face down on the floor, not more than five, feet in front of the door. I followed Hanley in. Babcock shut the door behind us.

Hanley asked Furnas. "Did you touch anything?"

"No sir!" the janitor said, rolling his eyes way up. "I didn't touch a thing. I just came in, saw her there, and then I *ran!*"

"Hmm," Hanley said.

"Hmm, hmm," I said. "Let's get on the ball."

Hanley sighed at me and kneeled down beside the woman. He touched the flesh of her hand and recoiled slightly in repugnance. "Cold," he said tersely.

"Turn her over," I said.

He turned her. It was plain to see that her limbs were stiff in rigor mortis. She'd been dead quite a while. When she was on her back, Hanley got up and moved away a trifle. I didn't blame him at all.

She'd been strangled.

She had brown hair and hazel eyes. The eyes were bulging, wide-open, a peculiar glassy veil covering them. Her tongue was sticking out, her cheeks drawn down. The brown hair was all awry. Her hands were clenched until the knuckles bulged like marbles.

On her throat, there were lots of thumb-like welts where the killer had caught her.

She certainly was a sight to see.

Hanley got to his feet. "She's been dead eight hours at

least," he said worriedly. "I'm enough of a medical examiner to see that. This is a hell of a thing."

"Listen," I said tensely to the janitor, Furnas, "what about this dame? Who is she, where did she work, who were her friends and enemies? How long had she been living here?"

"Two years," Furnas said, a little awed. "She'd been living here two years."

"What did she do for a living?"

"I don't know," he said. "I don't think she worked."

"How did she live then?"

"She had money," he said. "She sure had a lot of money. She got twenty-five thousand dollars from that hotel when she sued it. You read all about that."

I looked surprised. "Did I?"

"Sure, you read about that. You must've read about it. You know—the mouse in her meal?"

"Hell's bells!" I exclaimed. "Poppa, did you hear that?"

"What?" Hanley asked.

"This dame—this Cary Green—she's the one who was eating a creole stew at the Rochefort Hotel two months ago and found a stewed mouse among her mushrooms. Remember?"

"Sure, I remember!" Hanley said.

"She sued the Rochefort for twenty-five grand on account of that mouse," I said. "And what's more, she must have collected."

"Not from the suit," the janitor said. "She told me one night. She said the hotel paid her off out of court. She said they couldn't stand that kind of publicity."

"When was she paid?" I asked.

"Oh," the janitor said. "Not more than two weeks ago. She said she'd move from here after she was paid and she gave notice only the other day."

I murmured, "twenty-five grand for eating a mouse...." Hunches began to hit me. Poppa Hanley cornered the janitor and started his usual run of questions. Meanwhile, I caught sight of Cary Green's handbag.

And I went for it in a big way.

THE ONLY THING I found, other than lipstick, compact, some currency, and some keys, was a small slip of paper with some writing, her own probably, on it.

It said: *Call G.K. on Thursday.*

I slipped it back into the bag and snapped the bag closed.

"Damn," Hanley said, a few minutes later, "we ain't getting anywhere. This dame had no friends and had no enemies. Nobody saw anyone come today or leave. A nice job."

"A man did it," I said. "You can see that much."

"Hell yes! A man did it all right. But who is he? That's my job."

"Your job," I added, "and the taxpayer's worry."

"Okeh, okeh," he said, frowning. "Kid all you want. The fact remains we're not getting anywhere.... You got any ideas?"

"The one uppermost, in my mind right now is: Was Cary Green an honest woman?"

"Get the hell outa here," Hanley said sourly. "You get funny at the damnedest times."

"All right, Poppa," I said quietly. "Only you're wrong there. I'm not being funny about Cary Green. You couldn't be funny after taking in a corpse like that. I meant what I said. Was Cary Green an honest woman? I'm going to find out." And I left him.

The first thing I did was run down to the corner where I came to a drug store with a phone booth inside. I went in and occupied the booth and I called the offices of the *Chronicle.*

I got the Old Man again.

"Good thing you called," he said. "That Jordan guy has been trying like all hell to reach you. I think he's got a story or something: I'm telling you to get in touch with him."

"By all means," I said.

"You mean you will—without an argument?"

"Sure."

"You must be sick or something," the Old Man said dryly. "Then get this—Jordan said he would be waiting for you at your apartment. I told him to go there."

"Thanks for the hospitality," I said.

"You're welcome. Anything else?"

"I want the morgue."

He put me through to Charlie Adams, an old timer who handles the *Chronicle's* morgue and I said to Charlie, "This is Daffy. Get me all the dope you can on a woman named Cary Green who recently figured in the suit with the Rochefort Hotel over the mouse in her mushrooms. Savvy?"

"I savvy," Charlie laughed. "Just a second."

It didn't take him long. When he came back, he asked, "Want me to read all this stuff to you or do you want to ask questions about it?"

"I'll ask questions," I said.

"Go ahead then. Shoot."

"Who was the manager of the Rochefort?"

"George Kennedy," Charlie said.

"Aha!" I said. "A bullseye! I smell a rat."

"You mean a mouse," said Charlie. "Anything else?"

"Yeah. What was this Cary Green? What'd she do?"

"Formerly a showgirl. She outgrew that. Then a professional correspondent. She got mixed up in some mess here, perjury, it says, during a divorce trial, but sentence was suspended."

"Okeh, thanks, Charlie," I said. "Give me Brad for rewrite."

He put me through to Brad and I gave Brad all the dope I had on the murder and told him that there was more to come and then I hung up.

I GOT A telephone directory, looked up another number, parted company with one of my few five-penny pieces and called the Rochefort Hotel, which was located on West 45th Street between Sixth Avenue and Broadway.

"Hello," someone said on the other end.

"Let me speak with George Kennedy please," I said.

"Who's calling?"

I chuckled. "His Nemesis, girlie, his Nemesis!"

There was a wait of a few seconds, some ear-racking clicks, and finally a man with a deep, hoarse voice said, "Hello."

I said softly, "G.K.?"

"Yes," he said just as softly.

"This is Daffy Dill," I said. "The newshound. I work on the *Chronicle*. You know. You've heard of me."

"Well?" he asked guardedly.

"Cary Green," I said, "was bumped off this morning

sometime. I figure you know plenty about it. Do you get me?"

There was a heavy silence.

"If you do," I went on presently, "you'll see me at my apartment tonight within the next hour."

"All right," he said.

"It's on Forty-fifth," I told him. "You'll find it."

"I'll—find—it—" he said mumbling.

"You'll be there then."

"I'll—be there," he said with an effort.

I hung up.

3

THE KILLERS

BEFORE I LEFT the store, I ripped a page out of the telephone directory and I folded it neatly. I took out the letter which I had found in Vivian Merritt's bag and put the telephone page in the envelope.

There was enough gum left on the flap for me to seal the thing all up like new. After that, I folded the real message into the size of an abnormal postage stamp and I stuck it down in the heel of my shoe.

I left the store and I was going to walk over to my apartment when I looked down the block and I saw Bill Hanley and Sergeant Babcock coming out of the house where Cary Green lived.

I yelled to them and ran down to meet them before they drove off in the police car.

Poppa Hanley regarded me sadly when I came up.

He asked, "Where have you been, cluck?" and chewed on his cigar.

"Places," I said. "Find anything new?"

"Not a thing. Doc Kyne is coming up with the Public Welfare wagon to give the corpse a stiff going-over. But it looks kind of bad. I tell you, there's no lead at all. What do you want, Daffy?"

"Give me a lift to my apartment, huh?" I said. "And some info on the side."

"Clamber in," Hanley said.

I got in and we drove off heading back toward the west side. As soon as we were under way, I said, "Poppa, listen. Any word yet on Bomber Malone?"

"Not a sound," Poppa replied grimly. "That killer is someplace in this burg, you can bet your hat. But try and find him. It's no soap, Daffy, no soap."

"Well, give me this," I said. "Ever hear of Syl Smith?"

Babcock shook his head slowly.

"Syl Smith…" Hanley remarked thoughtfully. "Sounds kinda familiar. Ever hear of Syl Smith, Babcock?"

Babcock pursed his lips thoughtfully. "Uh-uh," he said finally. "No Syl Smith… Not unless you mean Sylvestre Smith. But they never call him that. They never use that name. They always call him Spider Smith."

"Spider Smith!" I said. "Who's he?"

Hanley grunted. "Thought you knew it all, Daffy. You just asked about Bomber Malone. Spider Smith is his right-hand man. A killer, too, but smoother. We can't get a thing on the bird, not even an income tax evasion."

"Hot damn!" I said.

"Didn't you ever hear of the Smith brothers?" Hanley said, "Holy, jeepers, Daffy, those Smith brothers were the two biggest shots in the Bomber Malone mob before Bomber took that rap. Spider Smith and Snake-Eyes Smith. Snake-Eyes is younger, more ambitious. He's got black eyes. They stand out like snake-eyes. That's where he got the moniker…."

I said; "The Smith brothers! Bomber Malone's men! I have something hot!"

"Fever," Hanley said acidly. "You and me both. I never saw such a night for killings. H.q. called me at the Green place after you left. Babcock and me are going uptown. Central Park."

I shivered as he said those last two words and I said slowly, "What's wrong up there?"

Hanley shrugged. "Patrolman fished a corpse out of the lake. A woman again. She'd been shot in the chest. Had a handbag with the initials V.M. That's the only mark of identification on her."

I shuddered.

"What's the matter?" Hanley asked, eyeing me sharply.

"Nothing," I said. "Nothing at all, Poppa. Let me off here. Last stop."

THE CAR HAD reached my apartment. They pulled it over and stopped it, and I got out, waved goodby to them, and watched them go off down the block.

There was a well-dressed man standing in the vestibule of the house. I walked past him, took out my keys, opened the door, then turned back and glanced at him again.

He was short, kind of dumpy looking. He had a red face and he wore glasses. I whispered: "G.K.?"

He twitched, startled, and he wheeled around.

"Yes! Yes! Are you Dill?"

"I am, friend," I said, "Follow me."

He went through the door. I pushed him ahead of me where I could keep my eyes on him and we climbed up to the top floor where my apartment was. We went in and closed the door behind us.

"Have a seat," I said, motioning.

He sagged into a chair. "Listen, Dill—for God's sake—I had nothing to do with—"

"Wait a second," I said. "I'll tell you what I think. I think that you and Cary Green filched twenty-five grand out of the Rochefort Hotel."

His eyes widened a trifle.

"Here's the way I look at it," I said. "You and Cary— maybe she thought it up—decided that if she were eating one of your super-elegant dinners there and suddenly found a cooked mouse in the meal, she could sue the hotel for damages and that you could exert pressure on the company to pay off out of court so that your hotel would not get a lot of bum publicity. In other words, Cary Green dropped that mouse into the stew herself, gave out a yelp of horror, and promptly started to sue. Right?"

He nodded dumbly.

"I guess you came in for a cut, maybe half, of the mazuma which the operating company paid her for damages— right?"

He nodded again, his lips white.

"Then," I said, putting the bite on him in earnest, "you got a little selfish. You figured as how you could use the entire twenty-five grand all by yourself, and without any help from Cary Green. So today you upped and trotted over to her hideout on East Forty-Eighth Street and you did a nasty job of strangling her—right?"

"Good God—*no!*"

"No?" I said, acting surprised.

"No, no, no! I didn't do it, I tell you! I can prove—"

"You can?"

"No, I can't prove it—but I didn't do it! I—oh, God!"

"Brother," I said, "you'd better give. Personally, I don't think you've got the guts to murder anyone. But that's the way it'll look in court and maybe a jury won't feel the same way about you that I do. Give, friend, give. Why—"

"I didn't do it, I tell you! You've got to believe me!"

I set my jaw. "Listen, Kennedy," I said coldly, "if you didn't do it, you know who did. Otherwise, you would not have bothered to come over here and see me. You know who did it. You know why. You're the only one. If you're smart you'll come clean. Either you sing right here and now, or I'll give the homicide bureau a little buzz."

"I'll—" he paused a long time, "I'll talk," he said finally. His voice was very low, very hoarse. "They'll kill me—you too—but, you asked—for it. I'll talk."

"Get going," I said.

He said, "Bomber Malone is staying at the Rochefort Hotel."

THE HAIR ON the back of my neck did a high jump and my spine did a hula-hula with the chills that coursed down it. "What?" I shouted.

"Yes," he said dully. "Bomber Malone is staying at the Rochefort. He came in late last night with two of his men, stuck a gun in me and asked for the best in the house.

"Then, this morning, one of his men—the one he kept calling Spider—told me he was going to fix me right. He'd guessed that Cary Green and I had worked the mouse racket on the hotel together. So he told me he was going to kill her, and that if anything happened to Bomber Malone—if I squawked and told the police that Bomber

Malone was staying there—he'd tip off the police and have me taken in for Cary Green's murder."

"Perfect!" I said. "Sure, what a plan… You were the only one with any motive for seeing the gal dead. No matter what kind of a yarn you gave the cops, you were all wrapped up for the chair."

"I still—am—" Kennedy said. He looked terrified, as though he were going to cry. "If you spill the beans—"

"That is a chance you'll have to take," I said. "Burnt fingers, you know, and all that sort of stuff." I got up and ran over to the telephone and called police headquarters. "This is Daffy Dill," I said. "Is Hanley there?"

"No," came over the wire.

"When he comes in, tell him to call me at once," I said.

I wanted Hanley to make the arrest, you see. I didn't want Halloran or one of those other birds getting all the glory. Poppa deserved the break.

I set down the handset and I started to say something to Kennedy who was looking very pale, when I heard a faint creak in the outside hall.

I snapped, "Start talking, and keep talking!"

Kennedy stared at me. "What?"

"You heard me! Talk! Talk about anything!" I ran to my desk and pulled open the top drawer and yanked out the .32 Colt revolver which is my very own, and I turned and stuck out the muzzle on a line with the front door, but I was too late. Kennedy had started to babble, but he was too late too.

Two men stood in my doorway, one tall, one short. The tall man was the one in the Tux, the one who had eyed me so oddly a couple of hours before when I left the Hideaway Club in the cab with Vivian Merritt.

The short man was dressed in a taxi-driver's uniform. I didn't need two guesses to know who he was. He'd killed Vivian Merritt, and the gun in his hand was the one which had done it. It still had the silencer over the end of the barrel.

The taller man had a gun too. Both of them were leveled more or less at me. The taxi driver smiled. "Careless of you, Dill. Leaving your door open like that."

"Open house," I said. "Everybody's welcome."

"Drop the gun," he said.

"Uh-uh," I said. "No droppee the gun. If I'm going bye-bye, one of you boys is going to show me the way."

"Drop it!" the taxi driver snarled.

"Hold it, Snake-Eyes," the tall man said. "Easy does it."

"Aha," I said. "The notorious Smith brothers." It was easy now. Spider was the tall one. Snake-Eyes the pug.

"Listen, Dill," Spider Smith said casually, "you have a letter which belongs to me. I want it."

"Oh, that," I said. From Bomber Malone, is it? Are things so tight that Bomber has to send you letters care of General Delivery? Can't you even telephone him?"

"That's right," Spider said easily. "We have to be careful. You know how it is. Let's have the letter."

"All right," I said. "Come and get it."

"Nix, nix," Snake-Eyes snapped. "None of that stuff."

"No tickee, no shirtee," I said.

SPIDER SMITH STARED at me a long time, then he stared at George Kennedy who was still sitting where he had been when we first came in. "Been talking, Kennedy?" he asked.

"I couldn't—he made me—" Kennedy faltered.

"Talking's bad," Spider said coldly and evenly. His eyes met mine and I smiled derisively. "I'd like the letter, Dill, but I think we can pick it out of your pocket just as well whether you are standing or on your back."

I didn't say anything. I kept watching the muscles of both their faces.

Very slowly and with utmost gravity, Spider Smith turned toward his younger brother and murmured, "Okeh, kid. Let' em have it...."

The words were hardly out of his mouth when Snake-Eyes Smith was firing the silenced pistol!

I dove down around the side of my desk the second I saw that it was open war. As I plunged, I saw Kennedy's mouth sag, then the blood rushed out—a black hole appeared in the side of his head.

I fired twice at the two brothers as I went down behind the desk but I missed, firing like that without even aiming. I heard the *ping* of the silenced gun again and there was a drone and thud as the bullet slid along the top of my desk and slashed into the wall behind me.

Simultaneously, the telephone rang. At the moment the bell jingled, I stuck up my head, figuring that the sudden sound would take both of the men unawares, and I was right.

They stopped firing for just that brief split second to turn slightly and stare at the handset on top of the desk.

In that second, I threw my revolver up to my eye, sighted it and fired.

The wind hissed sharply out of the younger brother's lungs, as the slug caught him just over the stomach. He gasped horribly, groaned once, and finally fell forward on his face, dropping his gun as he went, and hitting the floor with a jounce that shook the pictures on the walls.

The telephone kept ringing. I stuck up my head for another try, this time at Spider Smith himself, and just as I did so, he shot at me.

What happened, I don't know. I never fired my gun at all. I only remember the telephone ringing, the display of beautiful bursting fireworks inside my head, the three canaries in there too, warbling sweetly, and then a sledge-hammer walloped me hard over my left ear.

And it was sweet dreams.

4

THE HELENA'S GOLD

WHEN I OPENED my eyes, I saw Poppa Hanley's welcome pan with the drooping cheeks and bony nose right close to me; his mild eyes full of fear, his lips pale.

He was slapping my face and he kept calling, "Daffy! Daffy! Speak to me! You're all right, speak to me!"

"Cut it out," I said, struggling to sit up. "Never mind the slaps. Who do you think you are—Joe Louis?"

"Jeepers!" Hanley said. "You had me worried."

"Am I dead?" I asked, looking around. My head was going around in circles with the room.

Hanley laughed drily. "Yeah, you're dead. You're dead and gone to heaven."

"That can't be," I said; *"You're* here. Aoow…" I felt my head. It buzzed like a Pratt & Whitney. All I needed on it was a propeller. "What happened?"

"The way I figure it," Hanley said, "the bullet caught this little clock on your desk and pasted against your skull. You've got a bump over your ear like a watermelon, but no bullet wound."

"That's a big help," I said; "Thanks."

"Nice place you have here," Hanley remarked. "Nice and

cozy and one or two stiffs lying around to give it a pleasant atmosphere... Suppose you give, Daffy?"

"Okeh," I said wearily. "My head hurts like hell."

"You don't have to tell me that Snake-Eyes Smith is the one in the taxi uniform.... But who's the other corpse?"

"George Kennedy," I said. "Manager of the Rochefort—" I stopped suddenly and said, "How long have I been out?"

Hanley shrugged. "I dunno. I called you at eleven-thirty but you didn't answer, so I—"

"That's it!" I said. "I got hit when you were ringing here. That's when the fracas came off. What time is it now?"

"Quarter of one," Hanley said. "I drove up when you didn't answer. Got here around midnight. You've been out all this time and I've been trying to bring you around."

"Hell," I groaned, "we're too late. Poppa, I had you all set to be a captain! I had Bomber Malone located. He was staying at the Rochefort Hotel!"

Hanley looked at me dumbly. "You're kidding."

"The hell I am. Why do you think Kennedy was here? They framed Kennedy. He and Cary Green had pulled off a swindle against the Rochefort. After Bomber escaped from Wainsong, he showed up at the Rochefort. This morning, Spider Smith went out and put his thumbs on Cary Green's throat. That was a check on Kennedy. If he squawked, Spider would tip off the police that Kennedy had bumped Cary Green. Kennedy wouldn't have had a leg to stand on!"

"Holy jeepers!" Hanley said. "Then—"

"I'm not finished," I said. "You said you fished a stiff out of the Central Park lake, right? With the initials V.M. She's

Vivian Merritt and she was knocked off tonight by Snake-Eyes there and that gun on the floor is the one that did it!"

I felt into my pocket and I found that the letter to Syl Smith was gone. That had worked anyhow. Spider Smith had taken the envelope with the folded telephone paper!

HANLEY WAS ON the telephone, telling h.q. to throw out a dragnet, that Bomber Malone was in the city. I went over to my desk and took out the empty shells in my gun and put fresh bullets back into the revolving chamber. Then I dropped the gun in my pocket.

Hanley came back. "You haven't told me everything, Daffy. How about it?"

"No time," I said. "I've got to be rolling."

"I'm rolling with you," he said.

"No can do," I said. "But you can be a big help. Find out who Vivian Merritt was. Find out what her racket was. This is something big, Poppa, the biggest thing you and I were ever mixed up in. Every one of these things tonight, Vivian Merritt, Kennedy, Cary Green, Snake-Eyes Smith and his brother, Bomber Malone—they all tie up together. Something colossal is coming off—*and I don't know what it is!* We've got to find out, savvy?"

"I savvy. Anything else?"

"Did you ever hear of a guy named Jordan? W. Jordan?"

Hanley shook his head. "No."

"Well, by God, I never did either, and he's the key man. He's the one I've got to see. He knows the answer. And to think that I spurned his telephone call at the Hideaway earlier tonight! Listen, Poppa—see what you can find on him. His moniker is W. Jordan."

"Okeh," Hanley said. "You won't let me come with you?"

"No."

He smiled slyly. "Okeh. I'll see what I can find."

"Thanks, Poppa," I said. "I'll be seeing you!"

I LEFT THE apartment and I tore down the stairs. I waited in the vestibule a second and took a look around, but no one was in sight, so I stepped out into the street and I turned right to walk toward Sixth Avenue when something nudged me in the back and a voice said, "Get in the first cab we come to. No funny business, Mr. Dill."

The guy stayed right behind me and I couldn't see him at all, but I could feel his gun there all right, so I made no funny business and I kept walking. I asked, "Where'd you come from?"

"Never mind that. Don't talk. Here's a cab. Get in and make it fast. There's no time to waste."

Another voice, a familiar gruff voice, broke in at this point. "Hold your horses, mister."

We both whirled around and there stood Poppa Hanley with his Police Positive in his hand. He looked at me.

"I told you I'd roll along with you, Daffy. And as for you, brother, drop the pistol!"

I grabbed the gun away from the stranger and slipped it into my own pocket.

"Who is this guy?" Hanley asked.

"I dunno," I said. "He just came up to me and stuck this gun in my side and—"

"Just a moment," the stranger said quietly and quickly. "There's no time to waste. My name is Wayne Jordan."

"*Jordan!*" I snapped. "By—"

"Vivian probably told you about me?" he broke in.

"Not a word," I said. "She just told me to give you a letter—"

He clipped. "It's urgent, Dill. Have you got it?"

"Hold up your hands," I said.

He held them up. On the third finger of his left hand there was a ring with a small coiled snake on the crest.

"I'm Jordan all right," he said. "Hurry."

"Why'd you gun me?" I said.

"Couldn't waste time arguing in front of your place. Someone might have been watching. I was going to explain in the cab."

"Okeh," I said. I dug into my shoe and brought out the letter and handed it to him. "Read it and weep. It's all yours."

He snatched it from me and opened it and read it. Hanley still had his gun out. I could see Jordan's face pale and he muttered, "Good God!" He put it in his pocket and he said to Hanley. "Have you a car?"

"Yes,"

"I've got to get to the New York division of the BI of the Department of Justice at once," Jordan snapped. "Can you take me?"

"He can take you," I said, "If you give me a scoopy on this yarn."

"Done," Jordan said.

"Let's go," Hanley said.

WE RAN BACK up the block and got into the black touring car and Hanley jerked us away from the curb with a roar and started the siren screaming madly.

Seated in the back seat with Jordan, I said, "What's it all about. What's this letter mean? I read it but—"

"It's the *Helena*," Jordan said, as we tore south.

"The *Helena*?"

"Listen," Jordan said. "The *Helena* is the prize liner of the Marseilles lines and she's due tomorrow afternoon from Europe. Due to the strained conditions in Europe, the African war and the sanctions of the League of Nations, and Great Britain's attitude toward Mussolini, the *Helena* is carrying twenty-three million dollars in gold bullion which is to be stored for safekeeping in the United States until the European clouds blow over."

"Jeepers!" I cried. "I've got it now! Poppa—listen to me—who is Fergie in the Malone gang? Who is Fergie?"

Hanley said over the roar of the engine, "Fergie is Darrell Ferguson. He flies—an aviator. Used to handle Bomber Malone's airplane when Malone was a big shot rum runner during prohibition."

I said, "Does Malone own a boat?"

"Sure," said Hanley. "A sixty footer, fast as hell. She's called the *Aurora*. He used her in the old rumrunning days between Miami and Bimini."

"Then I've got it!" I told Jordan. "Piracy!"

"Right," Jordan said.

"What?" Hanley exclaimed.

"Piracy! On the high seas! Freebooters, loot, pieces of eight, and everything!"

"That's it," Jordan said.

I asked him, "And who are you, a G-man?"

"Operative of the Navy Department," he said.

"And Vivian Merritt?"

"Investigator for the Marseilles lines," he said.

"Man," I said, "my kingdom for a telephone! What a yarn!"

When we reached the New York division of the Bureau of Investigation, Wayne Jordan started talking to Special Agent Symes whom Hanley knew well.

Special Agent Symes took it all calmly. When Jordan had finished, he pressed a buzzer. Two more men stepped into the room. He glanced up at them and said quietly, "Get out to Roosevelt Field. Take Flyer Darrel Ferguson in charge. Set a police guard around his plane, then report here with the prisoner."

Then Symes picked up his telephone and said, "I want to speak with the Secretary of the Navy in Washington and hurry the call."

He hung up and pressed another buzzer and a male secretary stepped into the room while I marveled at the neatness and dispatch of the whole business.

"Yes, sir?"

"Radio the *Helena* at sea to change course for New York in order to evade attempt to pirate ship. Sign it from this office."

"Right, sir!"

"And that," Special Agent Symes smiled at us, "is that. Mr. Malone's *Aurora* will meet a ship tomorrow at eleven, one hundred miles due west of Ambrose Light. But he won't meet the *Helena*."

Poppa Hanley spoke up. "Say," he said, "I just thought of something. Mind if I use the phone?"

"Help yourself," Symes said.

Hanley called police h.q. and when he hung up there was

a red glow on his homely face. "Let's go, Daffy," he said. "I think we may as well clean this thing up altogether."

"What's up?" I asked.

"Bomber Malone's car," he said gratingly, "has been spotted in front of the Rochefort Hotel! I guess he figured that you and Kennedy, the only two who knew he was there, were dead. And I'll bet you five fish to one that Spider Smith is with him right now!"

5

END OF THE TRAIL

ON OUR WAY uptown to the Rochefort Hotel—after
taking leave of Jordan and Symes and receiving Jordan's
heartfelt thanks—we picked up a couple of patrolmen, big
Irishmen with gimlet eyes and pointed chins.

"Bomber Malone?" one of them said, when Hanley told
him the lay. "Bigawd, it's a pleasure, lieutenant, a genuine
pleasure!"

We parked the car on the corner of Forty-Ninth and
Broadway. Hanley was smart. He figured Malone and
Smith might be keeping an eagle eye peeled on the street
below, just waiting for some sign of a cop car. So we parked
on the corner and then headed toward the hotel on foot,
keeping in close to the sides of the stores and buildings
along the way.

"Poppa," I said, just before we reached the glass-topped
canopy of the hotel, "forebodings grip me."

"Meaning?"

"Meaning," I said, "that the roof of the hotel is on a level
with the roofs of the two buildings on either side of it."

"So?" Hanley said, eyes glinty, jaw set.

"So I take the roof. Let one of the cops cover the

entrance. Let the other take the back door. And you take the room where they are."

"Thanks," Hanley said drily. "Okeh."

"Listen, cluck," I said. "Here's what I mean. You bellow through the door. Make them lock it—barricade it—get me?"

"I get you. Then what?"

"Then," I said, "I'll fix it so you'll be a captain."

That's what we did. The two cops took up their stations. I took the elevator to the top floor after we learned that Smith had a suite of rooms on the tenth storey. Hanley got off at the tenth and aimed for the suite, his gun out.

After I reached the top floor, I took out my .32 and I climbed the stairs to the roof.

It was dark and cold up there. Below me, to the south, the lights of Broadway bloomed up against the night sky, pretty, gay. It was very still. No taxi horns, even. It was too late for that. It was queer, all those gay lights, and hardly any sound at all.

I walked over to the edge of the roof where the curved metal ladder of the fire escapes hooked up and over the side.

I leaned over, holding a rung, and I peered down, into the thick blackness below, illumined at various spots by the square patches of light which came out from those windows where the hotel rooms were lighted.

As I looked down, the shooting started.

It was far away, muffled, but I could tell it was shooting. Somewhere a window broke. Then a man yelled. Then three shots in rapid succession, and finally a dull chattering as a machine gun came to life.

I waited. In a few moments, one of the patches of light fell on the figure of a man, toiling up the fire escape toward the roof. I stiffened, watching him, and I tightened my grip on my revolver.

A few more moments, and he neared the top. Light struck his face. I could see it was Spider Smith. He was coming up fast, his teeth bared as he climbed and in one hand, carrying it loosely; he had a submachine gun.

Behind him: about one storey below him, Bomber Malone came, climbing up rapidly with a big pistol swinging in one hand.

I STEPPED CLOSE to the hooked end of the ladder and crouched low so that Spider Smith wouldn't see me until it was too late.

Next instant he came swinging over the parapet of the building and onto the roof. As he stepped over the parapet, I reached up, grabbed the swinging stock of the machine gun and with a nasty jerk, yanked the whole piece right out of his hand.

He froze stock-still, turning swiftly, and he stared at me as though he had seen a ghost. "Dill! For—"

"Skip it!" I snapped. "Over there, bad boy, and keep your trap shut or you get a slug. Lam!"

Pallid with fright, he hastily stepped over to the coaming of a skylight where he stood, his hands raised above his head.

Next, Bomber Malone, the dangerous Bomber, came over the parapet and leaped to the roof.

You know how he looked. You saw enough of his photos when he broke from Wainsong Prison. The round, soft face with the short black hair and thick, repugnant lips. The squat, broad body with the big muscles bulging inside his too-tight clothes.

Bomber Malone…. He stared at Spider Smith, whose hands stuck up in the air, trembling from sheer nervous tension, which broke without warning as he cried, *"Bomber! Look out! It's Dill!"*

"Up with the paws!" I yelled at Malone as he whirled around, his face drawing down in a gorilla-like manner, making him ugly and beetle-browed.

"To hell with you!" he roared and he started firing the big pistol just like that.

I let him have it with his own machine gun. He was too close to me for me to do anything else. I had the stock of the machine gun resting on my hip and the instant flame began to stab toward me from the black muzzle of his gun, I squeezed the trigger and fired.

It only took two or three seconds. Judas knows how many rounds knocked off. The slugs cut a line of holes across his middle, nearly severed him, and then he went down like a pitched rock and didn't move.

Spider Smith, meanwhile, had run around the coaming of the skylight, reached the roof door, and thrown it open to go through it.

As he did so, he came face to face with Poppa Hanley who said acidly, "Going some place, Spider?" and cracked him solidly across the jaw, sending him spinning back onto the roof.

Hanley followed him, his Police Positive gripped in his hands. Spider came to his knees, snarling and rubbing his jaw.

Hanley stared at him, tight-lipped, and snapped, "Start talking, Spider, and keep talking!"

"You go to hell! You can't make me!"

"No?" Hanley said in a strange voice. He glanced at me. "Come here, Daffy."

I came over. He took the machine gun away from me and he said, "Guard the roof door. Don't let anyone up here."

"Right," I said. I went over and held the door and then I watched Poppa.

Spider watched Poppa too.

Hanley glanced casually at the machine gun, then raised it and leveled it at Spider Smith's face. "Spider," he said icily, "ever hear of a guy being killed resisting arrest?"

Spider looked ghastly. "You wouldn't do that—"

"You talk," Hanley said, "or I'll fire. And I'm giving you three seconds."

"I'll talk! I'll talk!"

Spider Smith talked all right. And when he was finished, there wasn't a thing we didn't know.

To make a long story short—since you probably read all about it in the *Chronicle*—Bomber Malone had greased the warden of Wainsong for the crushout. The warden was convicted later on. The crushout had been planned for that very day.

Meanwhile, under Bomber's orders, his mob was planning the greatest act of piracy ever to be committed. It would have put the old boys to shame.

His boat, the *Aurora* was to meet up with Darrell Ferguson in Bomber's plane, and then the two of them, boat and plane, were going to contact the incoming *Helena*. It was recognized, also, that at the particular position where they were to contact the *Helena*, there was no other ship to answer a wireless summons within a hundred miles of her.

Fergie, in the plane, was to carry a fake torpedo in his undercarriage. The *Aurora* had a five inch gun on her bow. They were to stop the liner, the men on the *Aurora* were to demand the twenty-three million in gold from the ship's captain. And if he refused, they were going to threaten him with the five inch gun and the false torpedo.

It was smart. No captain, remembering the safety of his passengers ship and crew would have refused to turn over the bullion in the face of that plane carrying a supposedly deadly torpedo, all ready to launch it at the *Helena* should the freebooter's demands be rejected.

And the haul was a paltry twenty-three million bucks! They could have retired with that job.

Well, things happened differently. The federal men caught Fergie and his plane and the fake torpedo before he ever took off.

The *Helena*, in answer to the wireless warning from the New York division of the BI, changed her course to the north.

The *Aurora*, when she came up to the position where she had planned to meet the plane and hold up the liner, found a United States destroyer waiting for her. The Malone gang had the good sense not to argue with *those* guns.

Poppa Hanley got a captaincy out of the capture of Bomber Malone. They gave it to him last week.

And Spider Smith was convicted of first degree murder in the cases of Vivian Merritt, Cary Green and George Kennedy. Of course after the first trial—the Vivian Merritt charge—it wasn't necessary to try him for the others. He could only try once.

But this all happened a long time afterwards.

On that night when it all happened, I found that it was three-thirty A.M. when I finally parked me in a telephone booth and called Brad for rewrite and gave him the whole story.

Somehow then, I wasn't a bit tired, being kind of excited about everything, so I gave my one and only, Dinah Mason, a buzz and I said, "It's very early in the morning, Garbo, and I just thought you might like to know that I'm nuts about you."

"Well, well," Dinah said sleepily, "why don't you come up and see me sometime?"

But when I got there, she wouldn't let me in.

www.ingramcontent.com/pod-product-compliance
Lightning Source LLC
Chambersburg PA
CBHW030530030726
47495CB00004B/937